As Always

A BRIARVILLE NOVEL

BOOK ONE

EMERY THOMPSON

Created with Vellum

For every mom who thought life was too busy, but a book brought her peace.

Dear Reader

In this book you will find content that includes the loss of parents, death during childbirth, physical violence, domestic abuse, and off page PTSD. Readers who may be sensitive to these topics please be aware.

Much Love,
Emery

One

ZACH

I have always liked the sound of breaking glass. It is as if every shard falls and creates a unique melody. This melody however is dark and dreary and the tempo increases with my heart as it races. I don't even realize I have dropped the glass of water until Becca begins shaking my shoulders.

"Zach, did you hear me? I have to tell her. It is the right thing to do. My livelihood depends on it."

Pressing my left thumb into my right palm, I finally look her in the eyes. I don't know if she sees the tears, at this point I don't give a damn. They are showing my weakness, a weakness that only one person has had the privilege to see. She is lucky that I didn't throw the glass on purpose. I try to keep my voice calm but, how do you fuck up somebody's life so bad? "I will tell her! You fucked this up! You were careless and now her entire life is about to change." A deep breath lends to my self-control before I continue "This will break her and I need to be there for that. I have already lost so much. She has lost so much. If you so much as try to contact her, I will ruin your life!"

Becca cowers behind her desk, defeat spreads across her face. She knows that it is a promise that I will keep. "What about Elizabeth's family?" He voice barely audible and laced in terror.

The question sparks more anger in my chest. I slam my palms on to her glass desk causing the picture frame with a photograph of her children to fall. "I don't give a damn about her family right now. You have no obligation to them and if you inform them, you are breaking the law." I stand, straighten my jacket, and turn to walk out the door hoping the reference to HIPPA is enough to keep her quiet and I don't have to seek retribution on someone I actually care about.

Pausing before I leave, I point to her family photograph on the wall and I remind her of who I am, "I can tell you Becca, the judge is much nicer than I am."

I pop the collar of my coat to protect my neck from the cold October wind as I storm down the sidewalk to my truck. Anger pulses throughout my body with every step that I take, but fear also creeps its way into my head. Dread isn't something that I have experienced in my life that often, and I sure as hell can't let it show. I climb into the cab and loosen my tie, I hate wearing the damn thing, and my current mood isn't helping. Between my visit to the bank and conversation with Becca I have missed the majority of the day's work. So after allowing myself to break down for a few minutes I compose myself and start my truck. Garth Brooks' "She's Every Woman" plays through the speakers and I chuckle at the irony. I begin my drive back to the farm contemplating how I am going to fix this shit hole of a mess that I am in now.

Checking on my livestock will be impossible in this suit, but I know Aunt Celia will be waiting at the main house, interested in what happened at the bank and I don't have the patience now to deal with anyone else. I take the gravel road to the cabin knowing I have spare clothes there, and a pair of old boots in the truck. Once I am changed I jump on the ATV and head out to the north pasture where my men are checking on the weaned calves and getting the body condition scores of our heifers.

"Afternoon Sir," Andy tips his hat, "Herd is looking good, calves are doing well. Should be ready to move the herd to pasture 4 next week." Andy is young but my best farmhand. He received his degree in agriculture sciences at Kansas State and had plans to return back to Idaho and run his family farm. Instead he met Lilly, my younger cousin, who wrapped him around her finger and convinced him to come back home with her. They have been married three years now and have their first baby on the way.

"Great." I nod, the thoughts rolling through my head are not about my cattle. "Listen Andy, I need you to man the farm for a few days. I have some important business I need to take care of and it is going to take me out of state. You are the only one I trust with my cattle and my land." Guilt rolls through me as I ask him for more help but I know he wants the money too. I gave them some land to build a house so there isn't much debt, but they have big dreams and I know what it is like to want to get your girl everything she desires. "I know I have asked a lot since Elizabeth and Carter, but I need this bit more. I can assure you proper compensation. If anyone asks you, tell them nothing."

Andy nods in understanding. It isn't the first time I have asked for his help in situations that don't fall in his regular duties. He never pushes for more information, and always follows through on any tasks I give him. " Whatever you need, Sir." I shake his hand and jump into the ATV.

I prolong the trip to the main house by taking a drive through our racing paths. It has been a while since we have actually used them for their purpose. Garret isn't home much and when he is, racing isn't the top priority. The force of my foot presses the gas pedal to the floor as I hit the long stretch of open path before the sharp left curve. The wind rushes past my face and I smell the moisture in the air along with the crispness of dying trees and rotting leaves. The race of adrenaline numbs me enough to forget the chaos that just tornadoed its way into my world, just not enough to take it away. Nothing can take it away.

Mud and gravel fly as I skid to a stop in front of the house. I don't remember leaving the path and never slowed until I ended up here. Kicking my boots off on the porch I notice the dried tears on my face in my reflection on the storm door.

Shit! When did I start letting my emotions out? I am a grown ass man, we don't cry.

As anticipated, Aunt Celia is waiting in the living room reading her latest novel. When I enter the room her attention focuses on me and my demeanor. By the look of me, I am sure she thinks the bank denied my loan for the expansion, but it is the situation with Becca that has me pissed. Hurt. Without correcting her I take the opportunity to walk away and avoid the conversation, a look of understanding on her face. I head straight to my office where I know I will not be disturbed.

After 30 minutes of checking emails and pretending to give my focus to my newest business adventure I log in to the farm's social media page. Lilly actually runs the page, I am not much of a publicity guy and try to avoid any drama, if possible, but I do require her to let me have access. First, I scroll through Lilly's post about the farm and her research-based articles showing that we only use high quality products to raise high quality beef. Then, I do the same thing I always do when I am pissed and need the one thing that can calm me down. I search for her.

Stalking her social media isn't as good as the real thing, but it is close enough. Typically I am three glasses in before I scroll through memory lane to ensure I am numb as I self inflict my pain. Her photos and post remind me that I did what was best for her, even if it is killing me. This time I need more than just the calming effect that her success provides. I need to know where she is and what she is doing. I need to gauge how bad I am about to fuck up her world. Her status still says single which gives me a sense of hope, but also fills me with sadness that she hasn't found someone who treats her right.

Who am I kidding? She is married to her computer.

The posts that she makes show she hasn't changed much. To be honest she hasn't had time to change since I scrolled through her photos just a couple months ago. Her beautiful smile shines in each photograph, her long dark hair is pulled back in some, but when it is down it frames her face and her deep brown eyes pop. I scroll through more pictures and stop at one where she is wearing an emerald green evening gown and holding an award.

> "Dannielle Graham wins Woman of the Year. Dannielle has proved that there isn't a male dominated career that a woman can't do. Her programming skills have made a name for her in the tech world as well as the agriculture world. Her newest program is still in the early stages, but is set to change the ways of farming. Farmers are able to apply for a federal grant to participate

> in the studies that start in January. Read more about the study *here*."

I click on the link to read more about her achievement. It opens to a welcome video with Danni explaining the program and how to be a part of it. "I am looking for one farm to use as a pilot for my new program. In order to be considered for the program you must be willing to share business details with me as well as grant me permissions to complete my studies personally. The deadline to apply is October 31st and the chosen farm will be notified by November 10th. The study is a 2 year commitment and I will be relocating to your area during that time. You can find answers to frequently asked questions at the link below." Fuck! Danni is going to revolutionize farming and I am about to give her news that may change her entire life choices. I need to find a way to get her here, but she would never choose my farm and even if she did I only have 2 days to apply for the grant.

I was originally going to contact her today about the news. Instead I am pulling up to the main house at C.J. Farms for one last change to the business deal. Carl is having a hard time keeping up with the farm and his kids don't want anything to do with it. His daughter married a real estate mogul and lives in London. His son is a doctor and travels the world helping countries that don't normally have access to medical care. He is extremely proud of his children, and understands their need to leave Missouri, that is why he is selling. He is ready to retire and spend time with his grandkids.

"It will be in name only, Carl. It is important that I get to be a part of this study. When I purchase your farm I will be one of the largest in the state and the only one to have a focus in multiple areas. Your crop land only adds to my beef and dairy operations. The purchase won't be final until November 15th and the application is due in 48 hours. I will have Lilly do all the work and we will adjust the purchase price to include the benefits from the study. I feel like $500,000 should be enough to cover the time you will spend talking to the Committee, or you can also list Lilly as your manager and she can do that as well."

"I will do this on 2 conditions. Lilly manages everything and you keep the name C.J. Farms for this division of your business." Carl is clear on his wants, and I understand his desire for his family name to continue, but I am a businessman and I do things with my name on it.

I scoff, "Naming rights. You want fucking naming rights to a division of my farm. That is insane, I am purchasing your farm for over market value and offering you half a fucking million dollars to apply for a grant before the close of sale."

"That's my stipulation. You think the additional $500,000 is going to make a difference. I probably won't be able to spend the money from the original sale before I die. Take the deal or forget the grant." Carl is stern

I extended my hand, "Lilly and I will be here at 9:00 am for any information we need for the grant. Sorry for the late visit. I have very little time to work with." We shake hands and part ways. At least this step went the way I needed, now I have to appeal to Danni's heart and constant desire to help a hometown fella, as long as it isn't me.

Danni's hatred towards me is logical, but ill informed. What she doesn't know was that I ended things so she could follow her dreams. The weekend before our wedding the guys and I got together at Matty's, the local tavern, for drinks, my bachelor party. After a few drinks Garret, my best friend and Danni's twin brother, let it slip that Danni was offered a job in Washington D.C.. It wasn't just any job either, her dream job coding and creating programs for USDA. When he asked me how I felt about the move I knew nothing about I knew she wasn't going to take the job. She would never ask me to leave the farm.

I made a promise to myself to never be the reason she was held back and fulfilled it when I broke off the wedding. I still remember the lie I told her, that we had been together since we were 15 and I needed to experience life without her. I also still feel the smack that landed on my left cheek and the heartache I felt watching her move out of the cabin. She packed everything she owned into the bed of her truck and never looked back. She still avoids me on her visits home, which are less frequent now that her parents have moved to Florida and Garret is a pilot that can visit her often. She won't be able to avoid me anymore.

Two

DANNI

The plane starts its descent to the runway at the Kansas City International airport and I go over my itinerary one more time. First, stop for lunch with Garret before he heads out on his next flight. Then make the 90 minute trek to where I used to call home to meet with Mr. Jensen about the grant. It hits me hard that the first time I am coming home in three years is for business, but Garret is always gone and Momma and Daddy moved to Florida two years ago after retirement. I love my home town, but my ties to it continue to leave. There are only two people left that I feel guilty about not visiting, Angela and Aunt Celia.

Angela is my best friend, we grew up together and she also worked in my parents' bakery since she was 15, buying it when they retired. She has been with me through every journey of my life, even if it is long distance. It is easy to not feel as guilty around her thanks to our girls' trips once a year. This past May we traveled to Santorini, and spent two weeks escaping our responsibilities and embracing Greek culture.

Aunt Celia on the other hand is harder to please with my limited visits. I owe her so much and I love her dearly, but her nephew is an asshole and he is the reason I don't come home. Aunt Celia was like a second mom to Zach, which meant that she had been a part of my life since I was a kid. She never married or had kids of her own, but was very close to her brother's family. Zach's dad and mine were best friends, Zach and Garret are best friends, Zach and I are exes.

Aunt Celia is the reason I got into tech and farming. She taught me that a girl can do anything a boy can. Originally I think it was to get me to help with the farm chores, but later she saw my passion. She helped me find STEAM camps for girls and even paid for my summer camps when my parents couldn't. If it wasn't for her I would have never found my dream. I know that I will have to pay her a visit or I will never live it down.

"Hey there stranger!" I turn around to see my brother with arms open and a grin that reaches his brown eyes. His hair is cut in the same military style it has been since he was twelve, and he finally shaved his mustache. His uniform is sharp, he exudes confidence and power. I am proud of him for following his dream.

"How lucky are you to have a layover when I land?"

"I'd say you're the lucky one. How are you feeling?"

"I'm fine, flight was good. I am getting used to them by now, not getting as sick as before." The first time I flew I was sick the entire time and the following day. It isn't like I am nervous or scared, my insides just get all jumbled up. I'd say it is the equivalent to getting car sick on a long trip. Since I travel so much now I have found a few things along the way that help, and a few that make it worse. I absolutely cannot eat within the few hours before I fly, and I have to be sure to stay hydrated. Listening to music and working also helps, it keeps me focused and not staring out the window.

"Good, maybe you'll actually eat something then." He grabs my arm and pulls me through the concourse to his favorite airport food. The aroma is mixed with sweet and savory as we pass the many options along the way. We both order the pulled pork sandwich with a side of slaw, it is good but not even close to Ace's BBQ Shack at home.

During our lunch we tell each other our most recent stories about visiting our parents, he talks about his flights and the fun he has in between them, and I talk about my study. We almost make it through the entire visit without him mentioning his best friend.

"What is your plan of avoidance this time? He doesn't know you're here so he didn't leave like usual and it's Pumpkin Fest so you know he will be out and about?"

"I am hoping to stay at the B&B. I'll only leave to go see Mr. Jensen and once he knows I am in town he won't go to Avery's. I am here for business, not fun, so I won't be attending the festival."

"You can't be serious. Angela and Avery will never let you stay cooped up in that room while you are here. You haven't been to the festival in three years and they know it is your favorite hometown event." I hate that he is right, but I have a plan to help me stay unnoticed.

"Angela won't know I am here either." I try to hide my guilt behind a bite of food, but he doesn't fall for it.

"What the fuck Dannielle!" Shit, he's pissed. "Your best friend doesn't know you're home, and you think that is going to bode well for you?"

"Well, I don't have time for pleasure and fun on this trip. I am here to do work and fly out in a couple days. She will understand."

"I don't know if you are being naive or just plain stupid right now. These people have done everything to support you and you are just going to come into town like a thief in the night and not even say hi." My palms begin to sweat and I am pretty sure my right eye twitches. Guilt begins to take over, but I need to stay strong. It is a short trip and I probably won't even pick Mr. Jensen's farm.

"Even if you don't tell Angela, you sure as shit know Avery will, and you can't avoid her while staying at the B&B. The girl may be gorgeous but she has a big mouth. The entire town will know you are here within 15 minutes."

"So, we are still on that, hmmm." I take the opportunity to change the subject from my stupid choices to his. "When are you ever going to tell that gorgeous girl how you feel?"

"Oh look at the time, I have to get ready for my next flight." Avoidance as usual, clearly it is a hereditary trait. We clean up our table, say our goodbyes, and head in opposite directions.

Two hours later I pull up to the B & B hoping there is a room available. Mr. Jensen's application was submitted late last night and my team picked it for the next round. They think that going back to where my life began would be huge for the company, and I agree, I just don't think I have the heart for it. I could do it if I was going to be here for a few months, or even working remotely, but moving back for a minimum of two years is a commitment that I am unsure of.

I sit in front of the Dogwood Bed and Breakfast for a moment to take in my surroundings. Avery has done a phenomenal job with the decorations, the landscape is outstanding despite the fact that it is the end of October and most plants have died for the year. Based on the hustle and bustle of people on the terrace and moving in and out of the doors as well as the packed parking lot, I know that there isn't a chance in hell that she has a room for me. I also know that Garret does the bare minimum to mom and dad's house with his busy schedule and it isn't fit to stay in either. I would be spending my time here cleaning and organizing instead of working. I take a deep breath and hope that Avery has something, even a linen closet.

As soon as I enter the foyer, I am reminded of the reality of what Pumpkin Fest brings to Briarville and I am sure that there won't be a room. Aunt Celia is sitting at one of the tables having tea and reading the newspaper. Garret is right, everyone in town will know I am here by the end of the business day, that is if they don't already. I like the idea of visiting Aunt Celia without having to go to the farm so I step in her direction, but I hear an excited shriek coming from behind me. "Dannielle Graham?" When I turn I see Avery, the owner of the B & B and an old high school friend. She rushes in for a hug and my nose is filled with the smell of her fruity shampoo as her hair dances in my face from her jumping up and down.

"Oh my god, how have you been? I haven't seen you in what..... three years. What brings you home?"

"Take a breath Avery," I chuckle, "I am here on business. I am meeting with Mr. Jensen in a couple hours. I was hoping to get a room. From the looks of it, you don't have one though, do you?"

"I'm so sorry. Did you forget how busy it gets around here for Halloween? Pumpkin Fest is this weekend and I have been booked for months," she says with guilt on her face.

"It is okay, I can try a hotel out of town."

"That's just rubbish," a familiar and terrifying voice says. I know it is Aunt Celia without having to turn around. "You will come home and stay in the cabin and don't try to argue with me young lady."

"Aunt Celia!" I turn to give her a hug but she backs away. Her long silver hair is tied back in a braid, loose strands around her face are wind blown, probably from some work she has been doing on the farm. The lady will work until the day she is called home.

"Not until you agree to come home to the cabin." She is stern and there is no point in arguing. I have never won an argument with Aunt Celia and I know that this won't be the first. Instead I provide stipulations, she has always been a compromising lady, even though she will usually find a loophole to still get her way.

"I'll stay at the cabin tonight, but Zach doesn't get to know. You don't even get to tell him that I am in town. I have a rental car and I will park in the back. You keep him away from the cabin at all costs." Pride spreads across Aunt Celia's face and she embraces me in agreement.

"I hope you don't think he won't find out. It is a small county and he owns 80% of the land in it." she laughs and pulls me to her table, "Now, how does it feel to be woman of the year?"

Our conversation spans the next forty minutes as I dish the details from the Technology Awards. She tries to pry about my love life, but I am able to keep her at bay. After I finish my tea and carrot cake I leave to freshen up and settle in before I meet Mr. Jensen.

Three

ZACH

Lilly, Carl, Andy and I are sitting in my office. I have made them repeat the information to me multiple times over the last two hours. I need Danni to pick C.J. Farms for her study so I will not be at the meeting and I am not happy about it. If there is one thing my dad taught me it was that you take care of your own business deals and don't rely on or trust others to get the job done. This is more than just business for me though, I don't need the money, I need her. I also need Andy to continue running the farm as planned, even though I am still in town.

"Be open and honest about your family history and crop. Don't tell her that you are selling, she will walk away due to the uncertainty of the farm's future." I state harshly. Their annoyance with my lack of faith in them is spread across their faces.

"It is time to go Mr. Jensen," Lilly stands and stares at me, raising her eyebrow.

"Yes, you best get going. If I remember correctly, Danni

is always early and you don't want to keep her waiting. I stand to shake Mr. Jensen's hand and see them out the door.

I am continuing my meeting with Andy when there is a soft knock on the door. "Yes!" I am irritated that I can't focus and have had little sleep with everything going on.

Aunt Celia enters slowly, "Hi dear. Sorry to interrupt, Elizabeth's mom is on the phone. She wants to talk about Carter."

"Tell her I will call her later." I say without looking away from my files.

"Zach, it has been three months. She wants to see…"

I cut her off, anger fuming, "I don't give a damn what she wants. She has no right to my…" I stop myself short, arguing with Aunt Celia isn't what I need and it isn't her fault.

"I will call her in my time. She doesn't get to dictate when that is." Aunt Celia steps out of the office without another word.

Try as I might, I can't regain focus on the files. "You may go. Check pasture 4 again. Have the guys check on the weaned calves, and look into the equipment inventory from C.J. Farms. We need to start preparing for the takeover."

Andy stands to leave, "Sir, if I may?"

I nod giving him permission to speak.

"I wasn't here to see the grand love story and tragic demise of Zach and Danni." He pauses and I warn him with a stare that could defeat the devil himself. "But I do notice how this acquisition is stressing you more than the others. Maybe, just maybe you should lay low while she is in town or take Carter away for the weekend and really think about if this is something you can do for two years."

"You may go," I remind him. I stand to emphasize that I want him to leave.

IT HAS BEEN three hours since Lilly and Carl's meeting began with Danni and I haven't heard anything from either of them. At this point I am concerned she has turned them down and neither of them want to tell me. Cowards. I start to pour myself a glass of scotch when I remember that I have to make changes to the way I deal with anger. Instead I make my way out to the barn and saddle up my favorite mare. It is a beautiful night, cool but perfect for the Pumpkin Festival which I will avoid in case Danni goes. I ride until I get to the family cemetery, hopping off my horse and tying her up on the low hanging branch of the oak tree. Beside the tree sits the one thing that survived the fire at Aunt Celia's, a picnic table. I look at the heart with Danni and I's initials that I carved in it when I was fifteen. It wasn't like I knew that I loved Danni from the first moment I met her. We had known each other for years, but I knew from the first moment I truly saw her. First I stop at the tombstone above my parent's grave to pay my respects, but quickly move to Elizabeth's.

Elizabeth Turner
Feb 19, 1990 - July 23, 2021
Loving Wife and Mother

MY MARRIAGE to Elizabeth was one of convenience. My father refused to let me take over the farm if I wasn't married, and her ex boyfriend was abusive. She had tried to leave him many times, but she wasn't strong enough to stay away without a man to protect her. We made a deal, we married to give us both what we needed and promised to try to work on the emotional parts later. Eventually she did fall in love with me, but I can't say the feeling was mutual. I respected Elizabeth and I wanted her to be happy so I pretended that I did love her. We tried for two years to get pregnant, she wanted nothing more than to become a mom, and I figured she at least deserved that. Yet, here she lies, never being able to experience motherhood.

"I'm sorry Elizabeth. I couldn't give you what you deserved, but you knew that. You knew my heart belonged to someone else and you loved me anyway. Goodbye Elizabeth."

My anger has somewhat dissipated, but not enough for me to walk in and hold my son. Not enough for me to be around anyone, so I ride back to the cabin. When I arrive I notice a light on and smoke coming out of the fireplace. No one is living in the cabin right now since Andy and Lilly finally built their own house on a few acres I gave them on the east side of my property. It is far enough away that they feel like they are not imposing, but still close enough to be a part of the farm. That is why I have been able to use it as my own personal sanctuary when I am afraid to show my anger to Carter. I walk into the cabin gun drawn and I hear the sweet sound of a woman's voice singing along to Reba McIntire's "Does He Love You." I place my gun back into the holster and walk towards the Master Bedroom, as I get closer I recognize the voice. My heart races and I swallow hard as I quietly enter the room. I hear the water running and the aroma of a cinnamon spice candle fills the air. She's taking a bath. Fuck! I haven't even seen her yet, but my cock pulses just at the thought of her naked in my bathtub. I continue my walk into the room and notice the bathroom door ajar. I can see her through the mirror, her eyes are closed and her fingers dance across her collarbone as her plump breasts peak out of the blanket of bubbles that cover her body. I lean my torso into the door jam and cross my ankles, knowing I should say something but enjoying the show instead.

"Ahem," I clear my throat after a few minutes of torture.

"What the fuck Zach! Get out!" she throws the loofa at me.

"Get out? Get out of my own damn house." I chuckle "I get you hate me, but honey you're on the wrong land to be ordering me around."

"You're right, this isn't my land. This isn't my house anymore, but I am staying here tonight and this isn't your body to look at. So like I said get the fuck out so I can get out of this tub."

"That's cute, you think I want to look at your body. I want to know why you're in my cabin."

"Your dick tells me otherwise." Shit, obviously I want to look at her body. I want to rip her out of that tub and lean her over the vanity and fuck her like I have done so many times, but I didn't want her to know that. Why didn't I adjust myself before I cleared my throat? Secretly I was hoping she'd notice and want the same thing.

"Oh that, that's nothing. Reba did that." I try to play it off, but she takes advantage and stands in the tub.

"Well, I guess if it isn't me that got you hard enough that your zipper is about to break, then I guess this won't bother you either."

My breath catches and I throw the robe at her, "Put it on," I snap.

"What, do my breasts bother you? Maybe it is my ass," She leans over to dry her legs giving me the perfect shot at her ass. "Or could it be you miss tasting me, and seeing something you won't ever be able to have has got you all worked up?" She stands and walks into the bedroom pulling an oversized t-shirt over her head.

"What are you doing here Danni? Clearly Aunt Celia knows, that's how you knew the cabin was empty." I don't want to tip her off that I know about the farm grant so I play it cool.

"Just in town on business," she retorts, "I ran into Aunt Celia at Avery's and she said I could stay since the B & B was booked." She continues to torture me as she lotions her body. She knows exactly what she is doing too. This is part of her pay back, and she does it every time she is in town. That is another reason I try to avoid her, she wants to hurt me as bad as I hurt her, so she flirts and teases and then goes home with someone else. This time though she is in my house, there is no other guy to walk away from me with.

I sit on the edge of the bed as she continues to walk in and out of the bathroom. First she brushes her teeth, then she grabs her bottle of wine, then she grabs her jewelry, then I grab her. "Can't you just sit fucking still and talk."

"I can, but I don't want to sit next to you." She leans across me and I can smell the vanilla from her lotion. I lose my self-control, grab her waist, turn her and pin her to the bed.

"Listen, this is my house and if you are going to stay in it, you will not be a dick tease." I growl, but when her eyes snap to mine and she arches her back I feel the electricity between us spark. I lean down close to her ear and whisper, "As Always"

"Fuck you," She spats and yanks her hands from mine. "You broke my heart Zach. You left me, all because you wanted to whore around this county. I gave you everything, I was willing to give up everything for you and you just gave up. And worse, you gave up the night before our wedding. Do you remember the pain you put me through, laying right here in this fucking bed, you ended it?" Tears well in her eyes and my ability to reign in my anger drifts. I am not mad at her, I made her this way and I am about to make it worse.

"We need to talk. It is serious and I need you to put clothes on." I walk out of the bedroom and head down to the kitchen.

Four

DANNI

I don't know what just happened. I went from teasing Zach for payback to wishing that his hard cock was inside me. Then he said "as always" which was his way of saying that he loved me and it reignited the hatred I had for him; now he wants to have a serious conversation. I am going to need more wine.

When I enter the kitchen Zach already has a pot of tea going and my favorite bottle of ice-cold whiskey that I can tell was in the freezer. Shit, it is one of those conversations. I take notice of the fact that he has kept a bottle of my whiskey in the back of his freezer. The same whiskey that I always had back there for the tough times.

"Listen D, I am glad you are here. I have a confession and you're going to be pissed, but I need you to hear me out." I know he is trying to sound brave and stern, but I hear a crack in his voice, especially when he switches from Danni to D.

"Well, it must be important because you broke out the

whiskey." I grab the bottle and place it in front of me with an empty glass. I will be ready when the time to pour comes.

"I didn't know you were in my cabin, but I did know you were in town." He looks at me like he needs permission to go on. I nod giving it.

"You see something happened and I need to talk to you about it, but I also don't want to fuck up your life any more. Then, I was scrolling through your socials, and saw your photo from when you won Woman of the Year. I read the caption and thought that if I could get you to do your study here, then I wouldn't be fucking up your life."

He is rambling, which I have only seen happen when he is either nervous or terrified, maybe tonight it is both. He did fuck up my life, but I am not giving him the power to do so anymore, and it is important that he knows it. My guess is that he is trying to pull his puppet master strings to get his way, just like everything else he does in this town, but I don't know why he would want me here.

"I'm going to pause on the fact that you think you have the ability to mess with my life anymore and focus on the fact that you know about my study. Did you convince Mr. Jensen to apply for the program?" I pour the whiskey into the glass.

He nods his head and continues to speak, "You see I knew you wouldn't come if it was my farm."

"Bullshit Zach. If you had applied and it was what was best for the study I would have done it. I am not going to let you control my life anymore. I would not give up my life's work because my ex happened to be the best candidate," irritation fills my voice. I am confident when I speak, but it is total bullshit. There is no way I would have picked his farm, but when he says it, it is an attack on my integrity. Maybe he does still have the ability to mess with my mind, I mean I haven't found anyone since him that I have seen the future with. To be honest I didn't want to. I have fooled around, but always found an excuse to not get serious.

"I am sorry. I didn't mean to question your professionalism. It is just that I did hurt you and you stopped coming home, so I figured it would be best if it was someone else's farm for the time being."

"The time being?" I take a drink and wait for his puppet master plan to be explained.

"So not only did I convince Carl to apply for the grant study, I am purchasing his farm. The deal closes on November 15th. Before you get angry, let me tell you why."

"Ohhhh oh, I am angry already, Zach. You manipulated me. Now I have to decide if you are worth working with on this study." Of all the bullshit that I have seen go down in Turner Farms, Zach never manipulated me, at least until now.

"Bullshit, you know damn well that my farms are good for your study. You know this is the only farm where you are going to get work with such a variety of livestock, poultry and crops." He yanks off his hat and runs his hands through his hair. He is right, I know it, and as much as I shouldn't let my personal feelings play into my choices, I am.

"It isn't just the farm, I have to be able to work with the staff. Your farm may look good on paper, but I won't risk the integrity of my study!" I take another drink and wait for his response. He puts his hat back on and walks out the door.

I pour another drink and stare into space. I have already let Zach control so much of my life, but he is right. This farm would be an opportunity to complete the study with multiple different aspects of farming. None of the other applicants are so diverse, none of the other applicants allow me to give back to a community that made me who I am.

I grab my computer to email the board. I planned on flying out tomorrow, but I need to figure out if Zach and I can be civil enough to make this work. The only way to decide if that will happen is if we are around each other without arguing. If we can't make it a week, we won't make it two years. I selfishly want more time to fuck with his head before I give in as well. I click send and read until I pass out.

Five

ZACH

The day I broke my engagement I thought I'd never have children, especially not one of love. I had even scheduled multiple vasectomy surgeries because I didn't want kids if they weren't with Danni, but I would always cancel them hoping one day she would change her mind and come home, forgive me. Yet, Carter, my three month old son, lies in his crib as nature sounds play in the background to break the silence.

The entire day I have spent my time trying to avoid being angry around my son. I have done everything to help cool myself down that has worked in the past, but it wasn't until I was standing in this doorway that I felt relief. Hours I have spent avoiding Carter, when the fact is that it is him that calms me.

I felt Aunt Celia's hand on my shoulder before I even knew she was there. With her other hand she passes me a hot cup of tea and nods towards the hallway. I have so much to tell her, but I have never been the person who provides information without a plan. Right now, I don't have a plan. I let her lead me to the sitting room down the hall. She sits and I follow her lead. I avoid eye contact, staring at the family photographs and shelves filled with books. Generations of Turners have found solace in this room, but tonight I can't. After a few minutes of silence she starts the conversation in the only way she thinks won't upset me. "How did it go at the bank?"

I look at her, "We will close on the 15th. Carl has a few stipulations that I am not happy about, but it was the only way to acquire the land."

"Such as?"

"The division of the farm will still be known as CJ Farms." I take a sip and look away. I want to avoid eye contact with Aunt Celia as much as possible. She knows that this would never be something that I would agree to so there has to be more to it.

"Hmm. How did he get you to agree to that? Would it have anything to do with Danni?"

I almost choke on my tea, "Danni, why would you say that?"

"Oh I don't know, maybe because when I ran into her at Avery's she said she was going to interview Carl for a grant to work with her company. I know that Carl wouldn't apply for the grant if he had plans to keep his farm, definitely not if he was selling it. At least not unless there was motivation from someone else." A crooked smile fills her face.

"She wouldn't have chosen my farm."

"You know damn well that she would have if it was the best option. And if she didn't, you also know it's your own insanity that would have caused it. Now stop pouting, you're a grown ass man." Aunt Celia is the one person who I feel can always see right through my bullshit. My mom was blinded by her love for her baby boy and all my dad cared about was if I worked my ass off for the farm.

I stand and walk towards the fireplace, I stare into the crackling fire with both hands pressed into the wooden mantle. After a few moments I turn and face my aunt with tears in my eyes. "You don't understand Auntie. I know I messed up, but Carter and I need her."

"Now you listen here young man, you messed up. You should have left with her and you didn't. You can not make her responsible for you and a child you had with another woman. A woman you never loved might I add."

"You're right, I never loved her. I was protecting her, just like I thought I was protecting Danni." I press my thumb into my opposite palm, pressing down the tears as well. Then I unload the events of the day onto my aunt swearing her to secrecy.

It is close to three in the morning before I fall asleep. With the grant application requiring my full attention I have slacked on my typical end of month duties for my other investments. I send emails to the Dean regarding the internship programs I host on the farm and with my baseball team. Then I double check the numbers for Matty's, Joni always does a great job but I am a stickler for details when my money is involved, even if it is just providing help and not making income for me. Finally, I shut my computer and take the second baby monitor to Aunt Celia's room for fear I won't wake with Carter.

Six

DANNI

I didn't get much sleep last night due to the constant planning and what-ifs running through my mind. I have thought of every scenario possible and I don't see how any of this can play out for the best of the study and my company. I understand that Turner Farms is the ideal candidate, but will the partnership work? If history is any indication, it will not. However, I am going to try for the sake of the company and my life's work.

I make my cup of tea and enjoy the sunrise from the wrap-around porch. The view is mesmerizing, with shades of orange and pink smeared across the Eastern sky. It is also heartbreaking. This was my view for as long as I could remember, even before Zach and I moved into the cabin after graduation. After the rodeo accident I knew Zach would always stay on the farm and work for his dad, eventually taking it over. I also knew he would take his business classes at the local university to aide in his campaign to his dad. Mr. Turner was never the person to just hand something over,

Zach would prove that he was more than just a farm hand and had the brain and drive to be a business man as well. The university also had an outstanding Computer Science program so I stayed too. We were able to save money by living off campus and the farm was always our end game anyways. It was our start to making it our home. It has been six years since this was my home, but little has changed. I wonder if Zach and Elizabeth lived here, did they make love in the same bed that I picked out for our Master Suite. Did they cuddle on the furniture in the living room that we drove six hours to pick up because it was the only one left. I shake my head and shiver in the cold fall wind. I pull the blanket tighter around my shoulders and sip my now lukewarm tea.

I ARRIVE at the barn at 8:30 to get some alone time with the horses. I asked Zach to meet me here at 10:00 am, but I know he will be early. We were raised to believe that if you weren't twenty minutes early, you're late. Most of the horses are new to me, but there are still five or six that were here when I was. I walk towards the stall of my favorite horse, Kash. He is a gorgeous buckskin quarter horse that we bought as a foal from a ranch in Montana. He was the first horse that we purchased together, the first large purchase of our era at the farm.

I offer him an apple, scratch his chin then lean in and kiss his forehead. "I am so sorry buddy. I left you here with no explanation of why I was going. To make it worse I never come visit."

I know I am forgiven when he licks my face and I feel a sense of home. It is still early enough that I decide to go for a ride. "Alright buddy, let's get some exercise."

I grab the saddle but Kash is on the taller side, almost 16 hands, and it has been a while since I have been on this side of the farm, so it takes a little more umph for me to get it on him. "I'm out of practice, big boy. I work more on my computer than I do on the farms."

I hop on and we start our journey with a little warm up before I let Kash loose.The October chill stings my cheeks as Kash runs, but it is freeing. The feeling of the air in my face, the miles of open land, the smells of the farm all remind me of what my life used to be like. What it was supposed to be like. Up ahead I see the Oak tree near the Turner Family cemetery, and decide to break there. I hop off at Celia's Diner, a table where we spent many meals before the fire. After the fire Mr. Turner moved it up to the family cemetery. He told Aunt Celia, "It is like your home's own headstone. You can visit here when you need to be reminded of the memories within those walls." Mr. Turner was a great man, he cared deeply and loved harder. I tie Kash to a low hanging branch and walk towards the headstones for Mr. and Mrs. Turner. As with everything else, it has been a while since I have paid my respects. The fresh flowers tell me that Zach has been here recently. It was hard on him when his mom passed. We were sophomores in college when the accident happened. His parents were on their way back from Colorado with a load of cattle during a snow-storm. A car cut them off on the highway and they couldn't stop. The guilt Mr. Turner lived with after that turned him into a hard man. That was the day that Zach decided not to enroll in the next semester. Mr. Turner passed away a few years after I left the farm, the doctors said it was natural causes, but I think he was living too long with a broken heart. I wipe a tear from my cheek and turn to leave when I notice a new headstone I have never seen before. I walk over and notice the grave is recent enough that the dirt is bare from even dead grass.

Elizabeth Turner
Feb 19, 1990 - July 23, 2021
Loving Wife and Mother

I KNEW that Zach was married, but I didn't know that she had passed. I certainly didn't know they had a child. Hurt creeps into my heart. I'm not sure if it is for her, or for me. He ended my marriage before it even happened, ended a relationship that had been through so much that I thought nothing could tear us apart. We had been together for 10 years. We had established a home and began to plan to take over the farm. We had made decisions that 19 year olds shouldn't have to make because life threw us every twist and turn you could think of from death to cancer. Yet, he married her so quickly, so easily, and had a child. I sink to the ground as tears fight to escape my eyes. I don't think I can stay.

THE SOUND of boots on the dead grass and leaves brings me back to reality. I turn and see the look of agony on his face, wipe the tears from my cheeks and stand. My head is reeling and I am afraid of the words that will come out of my mouth if I speak so I untie Kash and mount.

"Danni, DANNNNI! FUCK!" I hear the shouting as I ride away. It isn't long until he catches up with me, but I don't slow down until I hit the barn. I jump off and hand the reins to the first farm hand I see. My anger is still fuming when he reaches out and grabs my forearm.

"Danni, you wanted to talk. Let's go to the house and talk."

I yank my arm away and keep walking towards the cabin. I know he will follow me, but damn I need the whiskey. I check my watch and it's 10:45, how long was I up there?

"Danni," he growls, "What the hell do you want from me? You ask me to meet you in the barn at ten, when I show up you're not there, then I find you in front of her grave. Now you won't speak to me."

The fact that he speaks about her like she isn't important infuriates me. I spin on my heels, "At least have the balls to say her name! You married her, and had a child with her. She isn't just a "her" dammit!"

"Now hold on just a minute. You don't get to tell me what to call her. You don't get to bring our son into this fight. Elizabeth was a wonderful woman, but you don't know our story."

"Then tell me, because there is no way I can stay here and do this study and not know. I cannot be around you and not know why you threw away 10 years of history and a future but were fine with settling down and starting a family with someone you just met." I scream as tears flow down my face.

He takes off his hat and runs his fingers through his dark hair then back down through the stubble on his chin. He sighs heavily and then out of nowhere in the calmest voice I may have ever heard him speak, "I guess now is as good as time as any. You'll need the whiskey." He passes me and walks into the cabin.

Seven

Zach

I HAVE BEEN STANDING on the porch holding the door open for what seems like hours, but in reality it's been seconds. Danni stands on the stairs with her hands on her hips, her eyes puffy from crying and her hair a mess from the wind and I still can't imagine anything more beautiful. My heart aches knowing I am about to crush her world. Finally, she walks into the house and straight to the kitchen.

"You grab your drink, I am going to start a fire. You need to warm up after laying out there on the ground so long." I head into the living room and start the kindling. Once the flames grow I start to add the logs. I can hear the clanging of the glass as I reminisce about our lives here. My last fond memory of building this fire was just before we decorated our tree. Danni had picked out the 'perfect' tree and she wouldn't take no for an answer. Garret and I had just cut it down and brought it in the house. She was in the kitchen making chili and hot tea to warm us up. I snap out of my memory when she enters the room and sits on the couch.

"Would you like a blanket? I can get you one from the chest." I want her to be as comfortable as possible when I give her the news. She just shakes her head, she doesn't want anything from me. Against her wishes, I open the chest and pull out my grandmother's quilt. It is more than just a throw that would be more logical for the situation, but it has memories. She doesn't acknowledge me when I lay it across her, but she doesn't fight it either.

"D, I don't know where to start. There is so much to tell you, but so many things seem less important now. I just need you to know that I didn't stop loving you. I didn't choose her over you and I know that it isn't what you want to hear, but it's the truth." She still hasn't looked at me, so I test the waters by walking closer. When she doesn't throw her glass at me, I sit facing her on the couch.

"I wrote to you, you know? I never mailed them, but I did write them. They are all in the safe upstairs. You can read them if you want. Later of course." Her head turns and confusion crosses her face. "There is no other way to say this but to lay it all out. Danni, I don't need your study." She scoffs and I clearly realize that probably wasn't the most tactful way to tell her the study isn't the reason I brought her here. She is the only person who never considered me an arrogant ass, but based on her response I know that she now does.

"That's not what I mean. Of course, your study would be amazing for the farm, and to be a part of a pioneering project would mean a lot, but that is not why I applied for the grant. I mean why I had Carl apply for the grant."

"Spit it out Zach or I'll pack my shit right now." Shit she is already getting angry and I haven't even gotten to the worst part.

"You see, about a year after you left, I met Elizabeth. She was dating some douche that kept hitting her and she wasn't able to leave. Her parents abandoned her, telling her it was all her fault and that if she left she couldn't move back home. He controlled everything she had, she didn't have access to money or a car without his permission. She tended bar at Matty's, but had to give him all of her money. Joni tried a few times to help her and when that didn't work I stepped in, I even let her stay in the townhouse, but he broke in, added more bruises and drug her home.

About the same time I was talking to my dad about taking over the farm. He was getting worse, making mistakes with the books, and hiding out. He refused unless I was married. I had come to terms with the fact that I fucked it up with you and there was no way I could fix it. So I married Elizabeth at the courthouse a few weeks later. My dad passed the farm on to me, and Elizabeth didn't get hit anymore. We both knew it was a marriage of convenience, and I told her that I could never love her, she fell in love anyway."

"Of course she did," Danni mumbled into her glass

A small smile crosses my lips hearing that Danni still thought I was lovable, even if it wasn't by her. "Anyways, years passed and I felt bad that Elizabeth couldn't be a mom, the one thing she wanted. We tried once, but found out that IVF was our only option for her to carry her own baby. Of course we went to Becca and started the process, eventually Elizabeth was pregnant, my son, Carter was born July 23rd."

Danni straightens and her eyes meet mine, I know what she is thinking before she says it and the sorrow in her eyes doesn't go unnoticed. "That's.... That's the day she passed.

Oh my god, Zach I am so sorry." How can this woman feel mercy for me when just moments ago she hated me for marrying someone else? It's Danni, that's why, the person who gives herself to everyone, even if it causes her own pain.

"My son is three months old and has never met his mother," I pause. "Danni do you remember Chad?"

"Of course, he isn't the douchebag is he? He had such promise. I thought he joined the Army."

"No, no he isn't, he did join the Army National Guard. Between deployments he comes back and works with Becca. He is the nurse that helped Elizabeth with the IVF." Anxiety fills my body, my throat catches and I press my thumb into my palm to help ease the nerves. She instantly notices, grabbing my hand.

"It is okay, Zach, you don't have to go on." Her voice is kind and calm, inviting even.

"I do D, I do," I sigh heavily as my heart races "Elizabeth died during childbirth. The doctors said it was hereditary, something to do with her heart. The doctors told me that I needed to have genetic testing done on Carter in order to be proactive. I consented to the testing, but nothing showed up with his heart. I thought I was lucky that he didn't have the hereditary defect. Then I got a call from Becca a couple days ago, saying that Chad saw the obituary for Elizabeth in the online paper. That he had made a mistake, and used the wrong embryos. You see the last time that Chad was in town was the night of my bachelor party. He went home early because he was leaving for a deployment and had to get to base the next day. So when Becca told him to prepare the embryos for Mr. and Mrs. Turner, he umm…." I stand and move towards the fire. "He um, thought it was you." I look at her and wait for what I said to register. I keep talking to ensure I get everything out before she interrupts. "He thought that your file just said Graham because we froze your embryos before the cancer treatment, which was before we intended to get married.

You see Danni, I don't need the damn study, I need you. Carter needs you." I plead

Eight

DANNI

It isn't like I never wanted kids. As a matter of fact I have always wanted kids, Zach's kids to be more specific. That is why when I received the diagnosis and my treatment options I immediately had my eggs frozen. Zach and I talked about it first of course, but it was the easiest decision that we made about the situation. A large family was always in our plans. That was until he ended the engagement.

There is so much running through my head: anger, resentment, fear, hope, love. My emotions are being pulled in every direction that I am not sure what I want to say next. Do I yell at him for keeping it from me for as long as he did? Do I call Becca and verify the information before I walk straight into that house and pick up my son? Zach hurt me then, but I know he wouldn't do this. He wouldn't make up this story and play on his dead wife's memory just to get me to pick his farm. My hatred towards Elizabeth was already at its peak. First, I thought she was able to make the man I had planned my entire life with fall for her in a fraction of the time that we had been together. Then, Zach told me the truth and I felt sorry for her. Now, she carried my baby. She experienced my pregnancy. She heard the heartbeat, felt the kicks, had the baby shower, designed a nursery. She stole this from me, and it wasn't even her fault.

The entire pregnancy she thought she was growing her own child. She made plans for her baby, she picked a name for a child that she was going to raise. She died giving birth to my child, she lost her life for a child that wasn't even hers. Here I go again hating and feeling sorry for the woman at the same time.

Then there is Zach! Fucking Zach. He has known the entire time that I have been in town, and he is just now telling me. Yes it has been less than forty eight hours, but he has known.Again, I know that the situation isn't his fault, but damn. I watch him lean into the stone fireplace with fear and sorrow on his face. Yet, I don't feel pity. I'm pissed. This is his fault, he didn't have to leave. This all could have been avoided if he would have just kept his promise.

I think back to the first time he saw me in this cabin this trip. He was cocky, horny, and told me he loved me. I was pissed then, but now it is worse. He was worried about his dick and emotions, instead of our child. He should have told me then, I should have already met my son. He comes in throwing around emotions and using the study to get me here, when he should have just called. But would I have answered? I haven't answered a phone call, text, or email from him since that night and believe me he has sent plenty.

There were emails listing my belongings that I left in my rush to leave, small unimportant ones like a book, robe, or other items of insignificance. I even received an email last week with an account number to the local bank and nothing else. I never got one about the embryos though, the ones that belonged to me, that produced a child that I didn't get to carry. It seems like his priorities are off balance.

I hear the shattered glass against the stone surround of the fireplace before I have even realized I have thrown the glass. I lunge towards Zach, screaming incoherently, tears streaming down my face. I don't know what my plan is when I reach him, but I want him to hurt the way that I do. He is quick and before my fists hit his chest he has his arms wrapped around me. My arms are trapped at my sides, but I twist and turn my body in an effort to get free. I fight until I am tired of fighting, then I fight a little more before exhaustion from the effort and tears take over. Zach's stamina outweighs mine and I don't know if it is because he was prepared for this conversation or not. My body goes slack and I feel his grip loosen, but he doesn't let go, he slides his arm under my knees picking me up and carrying me to the bedroom. I hear his voice, but not his words. I feel the warmth of the blanket drape over my body then the end of the bed sinks.

"I am so sorry Danni. I…" he whispers "I wish this didn't happen to you. I wish I could change everything and not be the reason for your pain." The movement of the bed lets me know that he is leaving.

"Please don't go," I whimper. My voice is hoarse from crying, and I am afraid he doesn't hear. When he doesn't say anything I curl my body into itself bringing the blanket to my face and sob. Within seconds the warmth of his hand caresses my face and despite the calluses on his skin the tenderness in his touch warms my heart.

"Please don't cry," he pleads. "Be angry, shit be pissed. Scream and yell, but please don't cry."

"I want to see him." I look at Zach, our eyes connect and for a moment a twinkle of happiness glints in his eye and the corner of his mouth curls into a small smirk.

"I will run you a bath and clean up downstairs. Then I will have Aunt Celia bring him to the cabin," there is hope in his voice, no, excitement. He leans in and kisses me on the forehead, and whispers "As always," and is off to the bathroom before I can argue.

The hot water is soothing, the smell of cinnamon wafts through the air, but I am still not relaxed. I am broken and I don't know if it can be fixed. My eyes are closed but I can still feel his presence. It is different this time, he isn't standing there ready to pounce like last time. He isn't horny or watching me seductively, he is full of guilt and sorrow. He is making sure I am okay and my realization of that causes more tears to fall. I hold my breath and sink down into the water hoping the pressure and quiet eases some of the pain. When it doesn't I resurface and see him holding a towel with a half smile on his face, "Your boy is here."

I HAVE BEEN STARING into the russet brown eyes that mimic mine for at least ten minutes. They are one of many similarities that we share, another being the thick coat of black hair atop his head and the olive tone to his skin. Although Zach's skin is a nice tan, it is from his work on the farm and fades a little each winter and his eyes are a deep green. In my heart I know that Carter is mine. There is no reason for Zach to lie, but I do everything I can to protect my heart before I accept it.

"I want to see a picture of her." Stunning Zach with the comment.

"D, why would you want to do that? You know it is going to hurt."

He doesn't understand, I know he thinks my jealousy will

rage, but I want to know if she shares any characteristics with Carter. I just stare at him until he pulls out his phone and shows me a picture.

The two of them are sitting on the stairs in front of a little white house. I recognize it, but can't place why. Elizabeth is beautiful with long red hair that can only be natural, fair porcelain skin, and green eyes. It is exactly what I needed to open my heart completely to the little boy in my arms. Before I hand the phone back to Zach I notice the sign on the porch, "Welcome to the Turner's," and the tiled address in the concrete stair.

"This is the rental house," I state, but it is more of an inquiry.

"Yeah. I let her live there. She didn't have anything to her name when she left that douche."

"I see. I also saw that sign." I need more information, but I don't know that I have the right to ask.

"Oh, that…." He squeezes the back of his neck as his eyes move towards the ceiling, "that is where we lived."

I don't know how to take that information. If he thought I was never coming back, why would he live in the rental property instead of on the farm. There is no way it was easy for him to be off the farm, which means he spent long hours away from home. I know his dedication to the farm, and the house was 35 minutes away. "Why?" The word escapes my lips before I realize I say it.

"I couldn't do it here. I have never allowed anyone else to live on the farm, not with me anyways. I did let Lilly and Andy live here in the cabin while their house was being built, but they slept in one of the extra rooms." He pauses and I can see the battle within, deciding if he should say what is on his mind or not. "No one has slept in that bed since you left. Even after I slept on the couch for weeks, then moved back into the main house. Sometimes I would come here to smell the cinnamon, or check the bottle of whiskey, stare at the emptiness in the room, but never once did I sleep there without you.

I don't respond, frankly I don't know how. I lean down and kiss my son. I stand, holding my baby close, when I begin to sing.

Nine

ZACH

Danni has always had a beautiful voice, and I am not just saying it because I love her. It is calming and powerful in so many ways. She is currently singing to our son and I know she picked the song with purpose. I know that she will instill the meaning of "The Change" by Garth Brooks into our son with every life lesson.

Her connection to music has always been about meaning and the moments in her life that she can connect to. She used to sit out on the porch reading a book, she'd come across a scene and think of the perfect song to compliment it. She'd rush to the record player or open up Spotify to play the song in the background while rereading the scene. Sometimes when she knew that "*there is just no other song that can do it justice*" she would play the song and make me listen as she read aloud. If she wasn't a farm-tech guru, I think she'd score movie adaptations of books.

The way she connects to music has also helped me connect to her feelings. It didn't get past me that she was singing a heart break song by Reba as she bathed in our old home where she assumed I was married to someone else. I'm ashamed to be the man who made her hate love, hate her home, hate me and I am going to do everything in my power to win her back. For me and for Carter.

I begin making a mental list of songs that I think she would play if our story was written. I want to highlight the happy moments, the ones that will remind her of the good times. There were so many over the ten years we spent in love. The one that meant so much is probably the one that causes her so much pain now. We planned on dancing to Etta James' "At Last" for our first dance. I wonder if she changes the station when it comes on the radio, or if she still has the vinyl I bought her for Valentine's day. Do these same songs bring back the same memories for her, and if they do, does she smile that they happened, or cry that they ended. Maybe both.

Ten

DANNI

It has been six hours since I learned that I have a son. My heart is full of love but I'd be lying if I said I wasn't absolutely terrified. I think that all new moms are faced with the "oh shit" factor when they find out they are pregnant, even those who have been trying. They start to second guess themselves, wondering if they will be a good mom or totally fuck up their child's life. The good news is that they usually have enough time to panic and get their life together before the baby comes, since most of them get approximately nine months to freak out. I had hours, I went from *hey you're a mom* to *here's your beautiful 3 month old baby boy,* with minimal freak out time.

Now I am sitting on a bale of straw with a cup of spiked hot apple cider wondering what my first mom fail will be? It is probably that I have had my son all of six hours and I needed to get away to let it all soak in, but also not tell my best friend who I am meeting at the Pumpkin Festival any minute.

I continue to analyze every option for how this family dynamic can work until Angela arrives at our meeting spot. Briarville is a small town, so safety has never been an issue. That is why this spot, on the northside of the gazebo, has been the spot that we have met since we were 11 years old for any important event, especially Pumpkin Fest.

"I am a little disappointed that I wasn't your first call when you arrived." Angela sits next to me as she pokes fun, but I know she isn't truly hurt.

"Duty calls, and I knew you would want to drag me out to this thing. This is a business trip, and you don't mix well with that." I tease her with a soft elbow jab in her side. Angela is the bad influence of the relationship. She has always been beautiful and confident, pushes me to take risks and live a little as she calls it. It truly bothers her that I work so much and have little time for pleasure.

"That is because I am the fun one." Her smile reaches her eyes, but then she stops like she just realized the place we are together. "Shit, does Zach know you're here?"

I answer her with a nod and take a long drink from my plastic cup.

"Well I might need to call in reinforcements. I don't think I have enough wine at my place to handle a night like tonight." She has no idea, tonight is not a wine night, it is whiskey all the way.

"Let's just have some fun. It has been years since I have made it back to enjoy one of these festivals." The rest of the night goes well. I explain the study to Angela and how it brought me here. I leave out the details of Zach buying the farm and Carter being my son. I haven't figured out how I feel about it all, and I don't want to be influenced by her. I love her and I know that she thinks she knows what is best, but I just need to do this solo for now.

The number of booths have grown tremendously since the last time I was here. About fifty percent of them are local businesses. Everyone in Briarville participates, even if your business doesn't sell typical items for the festival, you set up. You may have a game booth, face painting, or something you do has a hobby outside of your typical job. The other fifty percent are what we call circus sales. They are people who travel to festivals all across the country, they are amazing people with great talents, but they will be gone like the wind after the festival.

Mrs. Graves was a circus sales booth when she first arrived in Briarville. Her booth is full of old books where the pages are folded to make words or images. One day when I was 14 I found an old copy of my favorite book sitting on a table, no pages folded. She caught me staring at it and asked if I'd like to pick a design. I was saving money for a steam camp and just shook my head and walked away. The next day at the festival I walked by again, this time I saw the same book with pages folded to display my name, Danni. When I asked her why she just said that a young man asked her to make it and give it to me. He told her that if she made it for him, he'd have to give it to her and couldn't back down. I just smiled and walked away. The next day I was sitting in the bakery when Zach set the book on the table in front of me. "*Your nose is always stuck in this book.*" Then he walked away.

Mrs. Graves' booth is as beautiful as ever, and she has grown in her craft. The designs she has to offer are immaculate. There are intricate designs, words, animals, and even characters. One sitting up on a shelf catches my eye, a hummingbird. Hummingbirds were Mrs. Turner's favorite, and after she passed Zach would put them everywhere as a reminder. I don't know why, but my heart tells me to purchase the book, even if I am still pissed at him.

After Angela and I walk through the booths we find a spot to sit and listen to the live band for a while. They play cover songs of eighties and nineties music while people dance in the square.Soon they will be lighting the pumpkin wall, my favorite part of the festival. The local school gets a pumpkin for each kid and they carve it with the help of volunteers. Businesses and families also participate in the tradition of bringing their pumpkins to the festival and placing them on the scaffolding. Instead of candles a strand of lights is strung and a bulb placed in each pumpkin. Once lit the wall showcases a masterpiece that everyone in town collaborated to make. We celebrate as one.

"This is what I miss most about home." I sigh as I take a drink,

"The pumpkin wall?" She chuckles

"The community. Mrs. Graves came here as a circus sales, fell in love and never left. Even she knew this is the best place to live after 48 hours."

"I am pretty sure Mr. Graves had something to do with that. She was a young widow, lost her husband to a freak accident and was trying to continue their gypsy life together. Then she came here, had one look at Mr. Graves and fell madly in love. At least that's how he tells it." We both laugh, remembering the many times that he has told his version of love at first sight.

"There is just something about the little things in life that you forget about when you are married to your job. Everything I love was here and I still left."

"You were hurt, and you needed to get away from the reminders. You made the right choice for you at the time.

Don't get me wrong, I miss my best friend, so move back any time."

I just smile as I contemplate it and take another drink. They light the pumpkin wall and I use my awe as an excuse to end the conversation. If I let it go on I know I will tell her more than I am ready for. After a few more drinks, a funnel cake, and a few games we part ways to go home. I have had too many drinks to drive home, and I don't want Angela to know I am staying in the cabin so I wait until she is gone to text Zach.

Me: Spiked Apple Cider was delicious.

Zach: I am glad you had a good time.

Me: Did you read the SPIKED part?

Zach: I did. Are you asking me for a ride?

Me: I wasn't. I was planning on walking.

Zach: Fucks Sake. On my way.

Eleven

ZACH

When I arrive at the festival I see Danni sitting on a bale of straw sipping out of a plastic cup. Her eyes are closed and she is taking in the music from the live band, a cover of Conway Twitty's "I'd Just Love to Lay You Down." I don't want to scare her, so I clear my throat to let her know I am there.

"Isn't this a wonderful song?"

I think about how she connects her music to feelings, and wonder how this love song is impacting her now. "It is. Are you ready?" I don't want to be harsh, but I also know that this won't go well if I am the one picking her up while she is intoxicated. For the last six years she has flaunted another man in front of me if drunk, never has she asked for my help. To be honest she didn't ask this time, she made sure of it. It was her way of getting the help, but making me initiate it.

I grab her hand to pull her up, she sits the cup on the straw and wraps her arms around my neck. "One dance. I love this song."

After everything we talked about today, I don't know how to read her actions. I would love more than anything to dance with this woman. Anything to hold her in my arms the way I used to, but I need it to be a sober action from her. I pull her arms away and get her to focus the only way I know how, "Let's go Dannielle."

"OOOHHHHH he said my full name. He's mad." She chuckles and stumbles as we walk to my truck.

"I am not mad. I am trying to get you home without pissing you off."

"Sound mad to me. Big meanie won't even dance with the mother of his child."

"Fuck, Danni, how much have you had to drink?"

"Not enough to forget that the man who broke my heart is now the father of my child. Or enough to forget that he told me he loved me with a hard on even though he is the one that destroyed our relationship."

"All right. That's enough." I don't fight trying to get her to walk anymore. I pick her up and throw her over my shoulder and haul her drunk ass to my truck. She slaps my ass and mumbles something incoherent. I am sure it has something to do with another way that I fucked up.

The drive to the cabin isn't long, but Danni still passed out on the way there. I lift her out of the truck and carry her to the bedroom. I grab her bag and dig out her phone to put it on the charger. I grab a bottle of water and some Aleve to put on the nightstand. She is going to have a rough morning, and I need all the help I can get to win some brownie points.

After I get back to the main house I get on the computer to look through her socials. She is the most organized person I know and her photo albums are sorted by years, then events. I scroll back to the years we were together and find that she didn't delete the memories. I open the folder from 2013. We were 22 years old and Danni had been cancer free for 18 months. I had wanted to propose the day I turned 18, but my mom told me I needed to wait. To let Danni make her life choices first without being tied to Briarville. When she was diagnosed, I wanted to propose then, but Danni said she wanted to be cancer free and didn't want me tied down to someone who could die.

This trip was it. Eighteen months cancer free, Danni was about to graduate college despite her treatments, and we were in Ireland. Danni had always wanted to visit and her parents made it happen.

The pictures don't do the beautiful country justice. The vastness of green and beauty was only matched by Danni herself. I can still see the joy in her eyes, the moment she felt that we finally made it. We were going to start our lives together and nothing could stop us, not even cancer. Yet, I did. I stopped it. Fuck, I am an idiot.

Before I go to bed, I text Danni. I know she won't see it until the morning, but I want her to be thinking about the farm and making it work, not what happened tonight. Her hangover will be enough of a reminder.

Me: Cattle auction in 6 days. Trial run?

Twelve

ZACH

Gentle isn't a word that many use to describe me, but I wouldn't say that ruthless is either. However, it wouldn't be true if I told you that I have never used force to protect the people I care about. Shit, I barely knew Elizabeth the first time I had an altercation with that douche ex of hers. I have also made it known you don't mess with my business. About three years ago there were a few fools that decided they wanted to destroy some of my crops by riding their ATVs through my field, they also caused a few bloody knuckles and a night in jail. It isn't a side of me that I like, but I know it is there and so do others. That is why I use it sometimes, hoping the threat is enough to keep trouble at bay.

The last time I was here I threatened Becca, as soon as I left I hated myself. Becca has been a positive person in my life as well as Danni's. She helped navigate the waters when we were facing the diagnosis and planning our future. She helped give Elizabeth something she couldn't. Yet, here I am playing the asshole again, making sure she doesn't contact Elizabeth's family.

I don't even stop at reception when I walk in, I saunter to her office door and open it without knocking. It's a dick move, but appearances have to be kept. The fear in her eyes is evident as soon as she sees me. Her body stiffens and her hands tighten on the folder that she is reviewing. Vile rises in my throat at the sight of it, but I keep my composure.

"Good morning," she questions.

"This is a courtesy visit, Becca," I stand with my hands in my vest pocket, my hat stays on my head, I am showing no mercy or respect. "Danni knows, but Elizabeth's family doesn't." I see her shoulders relax and then stiffen again. She begins to speak but I cut her off. "It stays that way until I am ready to change it."

"She was my friend Zach." Sadness coats her words, "They keep contacting me. They want my help to see him because you won't answer."

"I would answer Becca. I would answer if he was their fucking grandson. I would answer if you and Chad didn't fuck up their life. I would answer if it wasn't going to break them that their daughter died giving birth to a child that wasn't fucking hers. Let's be honest though, do they even miss her? They threw her away, let that piece of shit excuse of a man beat her to near death and blamed her. Forgive me if I don't care about their feelings right now. They only cared about her because of the baby she was carrying, the money that she married into, and their benefit. So fuck them!" The pace and volume of my voice increases with each sentence as I close the distance between me and her desk.

"If you tell them," I sigh and my shoulders meet my ears before dropping again, "Well, you remember what will happen. Don't make me do it Becca." Then I leave the office, but the vile returns to my throat.

The drive across the county to Elizabeth's parent's house is quiet, music is playing in the background but the thoughts in my head drown it out. They treated Elizabeth like shit so they don't deserve Carter even if he was their grandchild, but I know it will still hurt for them to know he isn't.

Her dad is working in the garage as I pull into the drive. It hits him who is here and he perks up, a smile crosses his face and he hollers for his wife. I hear the creek of the screen door before I see her standing there. They think I have Carter, but they stop in their tracks when I don't open the back door. Confusion covers their faces as I move towards them. I speak up before either has a chance, "Afternoon. Carter isn't here. I know you have waited and I know you want to see him, but there is something I need to say." I am filled with both pity and anger. "Elizabeth was a wonderful woman. She was strong and brave and deserved a life full of love and motherhood." The confusion changes to embarrassment, shame and maybe a bit of sorrow. I don't know that these people know how to love, so how can they be sad about what they have lost.

"Carter is my son, not yours. You have no rights to him."

"He is our grandson!" Anger laces her father's voice.

"But that's it, he isn't. Carter's grandparents are buried next to your daughter, in a family cemetery on my land, that you will never step foot on again. You didn't deserve Elizabeth; you don't deserve Carter."

"How dare you!" Her mom lunges at me, but my quickness removes me from her aim.

"He isn't Elizabeth's son," calmness is still prevalent even in my rage. "There was a mistake made at the clinic. The nurse used the wrong eggs."

"That isn't possible!"

"It is, you see I was ready to propose to the love of my life when she was diagnosed with cancer. We froze her eggs in order to protect them from the radiation and chemotherapy. Those were the eggs that were used. Your daughter carried Dannielle Graham's baby. I found out just five days ago, Danni found out three days ago."

"No, this can't be. She loved you. She loved Carter."

"She did, but you didn't love her. Carter will know his mom and her family. Carter will most likely move to Washington with his mom. You have no rights. Stop contacting my family and don't step foot on my land."

I step into the cab and drive away. In my rearview mirror I see them still standing, not moving, stunned by my demands, knowing the promise my words mean.

It takes a good 25 minutes to get out of my funk from being a dick to both Becca and Elizabeth's family, but I know that I need to change my mood before calling Carl. He will be glad to know that he doesn't have to be a part of the grant anymore. To do so I stop by the bakery and grab a cup of coffee.

Angela looks up when the bell rings above the door and smiles, but it isn't as welcoming as the ones I got six years ago. After Danni left, Angela blamed me and rightfully so. Her best friend left, but worse than that I broke her heart. Eventually, she let me back in the bakery to get my own coffee and desserts. It was probably a year that I had to send Lilly.

"You look a little pissy. Did you find out Danni was in town?"

"Yeah, but that's not it. It is Elizabeth's parents." I point to the display case, "I'll take the oatmeal scotchie, a black coffee, and a dozen of the raspberry macarons. Don't worry I will let Aunt Celia give them to her." I don't know if Angela knows Danni is staying at the cabin, I assume not since she didn't ask her to bring her home from the festival. She just rolls her eyes.

"For not loving someone you sure do go out of your way a lot."

"Who ever said I didn't love her? But please, I came here to help my mood and not make it worse."

"Then you came to the right place, it's on the house today. I'll see you tomorrow for breakfast. Do you want the same snack for the auction next week?"

"Yeah, see you then. Thanks again Ang."

The cookie and coffee curb my shitty mood a bit, but the real trick is sitting on the tailgate staring into the water. I don't remember the last time I went fishing, but just being close to the water takes away some tension. The first time I came here and many times after that it was with my dad. Yes we would fish, but sometimes we just sat and talked. It was his way of coping and relieving stress and something I was happy to share with him.

At this point in my life I don't make it out here enough, but since Carter arrived I made myself a promise to try and calm my shit before I walked through the doors to him. Also, I can't wait to share this spot with him. Thinking about all the great things I want to pass down to him reminds me that I need to find a way for Danni to stay here, at least for the study. Then I have two years to convince her into forever.

Carl picks up after the fourth ring. "This is Carl." His gruff voice travels through my phone.

"Carl, I have some news, I think you are going to like it."

"Did you get the grant? I knew you would."

"I haven't yet, but I did tell Danni the truth about buying your farm and the bank says we can close today. A deal is a deal and I'll keep up my end of the bargain, the entity will still be called "CJ Farms," but you don't have to deal with anything else. You are good to head to London. You can become a proper gentleman now." I snicker.

"Well there is no point in changing my plan, I've still gotta get my junk out of the main house and I have a couple meetings with a few folks about my old cars. So, if you need anything you just let me know. I'm leaving on November 18th."

"Would one of those old cars be that ol' 1967 Fastback?"

"I do have that one and the '54 Chevy 3100. You interested?"

"Not the truck, just the Mustang. I have an ol' friend I need to apologize to and maybe if I get it to her standards, I can climb my way out of a deep ass hole."

"Why don't you stop on over tonight after you check your pasture and we can figure something out. I don't know that the car will save your ass, but Danni sure deserves it either way."

Carl isn't wrong, I'll be lucky if she even thinks about forgiving me, elated if she does. The Mustang has a bit of work to be done, and I'll need Garret to help. Fixing old cars was always our therapy when shit got real. Broken hearts, big games that didn't go our way, the loss of my parents, so many topics of conversations with an orchestra of power tools in the background. The real trick will be hiding the reason from Garret and Garret from Danni. If she knows he is in town I will never get a minute of his time.

IT HAS BEEN five days since Danni first held our son. Five days of bonding, bath times, giggles, stories and songs. It has also been five nights of midnight diaper changes, feedings, and cuddles. She is the mom I always knew that she would be.

Since then we have made one of the extra rooms in the cabin a nursery so Carter can be near Danni. I have been sleeping on the couch, because as much as I want her to have him, I also want to be with him, but my 6' 3" body doesn't like it. I am trying not to overstep or force myself into her life than I already have, but I want to ask her if it is okay to stay in the cabin. I can use one of the guest rooms, if only I had the balls to ask her.

We adjusted the office to meet her needs for now. She told me that she still has to review all the applications for the grant and that she can't just pick my farm because of Carter. She has integrity and a reputation to protect and I know that is important, but I'd be lying if I didn't wish she'd just stay.

The entire plan was to get her to pick my farm then tell her about our son. I knew that she would always wonder if she did what was right, or picked with her heart if she knew about Carter first. It is just another way I have fucked up and made her life harder than it needed to be. I guess that is one thing she can always count on from me, a difficult life. It is something I need to change though, I am hoping that starts today.

We are doing some more work to see if the farm is going to be what is best for the study, and that means we are headed to the cattle auction. It will be a long trip, a six hour drive one way, so Carter is staying with Aunt Celia and Danni and I will have ample time to talk. I know my approach to everything will determine the outcome of the grant dedication, so I need to stick to Turner Farm business, and leave the personal shit at home.

I toss our bags into the cab of the truck, I include the

basket full of snacks and books that I threw together. I make sure to include a pillow and Grandma's quilt for Danni to nap. I don't know if much has changed but I predict this ride to be similar to the past. For the first hour or so Danni will mess with the radio and snack like a child on their way to Disney. Then, she will open up her laptop and get down to business, research, coding, probably grant work. Once her brain has reached max workload capacity she will throw in her airpods and listen to an audio book, falling asleep. Even after six years, I'd be willing to bet the farm on it.

After everything is loaded and ready for the road I head inside to say goodbye to Aunt Celia and Carter. I stop when I hear the conversation taking place in the other room.

"Maybe I shouldn't go. I just met him. He is too young to be away from his parents. We could take him, I don't want him to be too much for you Auntie." Danni rushes through the words, anxiety evident.

"Honey pot, who do you think has been taking care of these boys?" Aunt Celia chuckles.

"Zachary is enough work for you this weekend, Carter will be just fine. Now you go and hit the road. Remember that you have worked hard to get where you are and Carter doesn't change that. You don't have to give it up if this isn't the right farm. Carter is yours, forever. You are his momma and Zach knows that."

Aunt Celia isn't trying to convince her not to pick the farm. If you knew Auntie, she is actually doing the exact opposite in her own weird way. She has more confidence that Danni will stay than I do, but I have to remind myself that she has more at stake than I do. Her reassurance that Danni doesn't need to pick the farm will actually be what Danni needs to feel right about picking it, and Auntie knows that.

I tap my knuckles on the entry to the living area, "Better

hit the restroom before we head out." A smile reaches my eyes when I reach for Carter. "I'll take him, I need some of those baby sugars before we leave." Danni is hesitant to hand him over, but it isn't because she doesn't trust me, it's that she has already missed so much time, she wants to soak it all in.

Once Carter is in my arms Danni rushes to the restroom. Her trip is quick and she comes rushing back out to give Carter one last kiss before we walk out the door. The walk to the truck is a bit quiet and awkward, but spirits lift a bit when Danni sees the snacks I have packed for her.

The entire trip feels like an FBI interrogation. What changes have I made to the farm since she left? What do I produce? Am I willing to let her make changes as needed for the study? Sometimes I can tell she is wondering if I am just giving her the answers that she wants to hear, or telling the truth. I don't take offense, I know that she knows how the Turners do business and let's be frank, letting someone outside the family isn't a part of it. Danni isn't just anybody though, she's family even if it isn't the way it was supposed to happen. I feel like this trip is exactly what I needed to convince her to pick Turner Farms for the farm and not because of Carter, he is an added bonus.

Thirteen

DANNI

The trip with Zach was informative and strictly business. It was a great test of our abilities to stay in the roles we need. There were times we talked about Carter, but never our relationship. He didn't push me, or even flirt which reiterated that his sacrifice of letting Carl keep his name on the farm was to bring Carter his mom. All of this was great news, but it didn't stop my heart from racing when he was near, when he picked a restaurant that he knew I would love, but he wasn't a fan of for dinner, or when I noticed all travel snacks and *necessities* he packed because he remembered all my weird travel habits. That is why I am sitting at Matty's.

Matty's is the local hole in the wall. A wide range of music plays from the electronic jukebox on the back wall surrounded by signatures of both local celebrities and any real ones that ever pass through. The decor ranges from vintage beer lights and signs to local and regional sports regalia. Every new championship from the high school to professionals gets displayed along with every version of retired jerseys from the high school's teams.

The bar is empty except for me and a few retired men who meet and play pitch everyday at three. Honestly, I am surprised they are here this late, soon the crowds will start rolling in and when Angela gets here I will have to change my tone from "worried the torch I still carry for my ex will burn me right up" to "fun girls night with my best friend."

I'm ordering another beer when I feel a gust of wind from the door opening which pulls my attention to the person walking through it. I tap the bar "make that two, and add a couple shots," then I am off the stool running into the arms of my brother. I wrap my arms around him with a squeal.

"Whoa, Sis." Garret holds me out at arm's length taking in my outfit. "Don't you think you are a little overdressed for this old place?"

"It's girl's night. How will I get free drinks if I don't flaunt it?" I spin around and flip my long dark curls to help exaggerate my point. When I am facing my brother again I see he is a little more rigid.

"Does that mean Avery is coming too?" My brother has always had a thing for her, but says that he can't make her happy being gone all the time so he doesn't try.

"Sure is, Ang and her should be here any moment. You want me to put in a good word for you?" I jab him with my elbow as I lead him to the bar.

"I can tell I am going to need that shot." A smile crosses his face, but I see the contemplation in his eyes. This is the first time he has never instantly said no, even when I am joking. Traveling must be wearing on his lonely heart.

"So, when did you get back in town? And why wasn't I your first stop?"

"About an hour ago, and you were. Why else do you think

I showed up here? I stopped at the cabin and when you weren't there I found Celia in the greenhouse. She told me about the trip and I knew you'd be here over analyzing everything."

My brother is absolutely right. It is just the way my brain works, but tonight I wasn't just over analyzing things. I was trying to drown them out. As soon as I got home from the trip I spent a few hours with Carter, but then hopped in the shower and dressed in my favorite sage green dress. I texted my friends and told them that I needed a girls night that included drinks and a random hot dance partner. Our town isn't the typical place that we like to go, but I didn't want to be out too late and leave all things Carter just to Zach. It wasn't fair to him or Aunt Celia which I know will be watching Carter if Zach finds out Garret is in town and not hanging out with him. I'm actually stunned he doesn't already know, they have this weird bromance intuition going on where you'd think Garret was his twin and not mine.

"Actually, I am here for a good time tonight. Not to think about Zach at all." I try to hide my lie from being displayed all over my face by taking a long drink of my beer.

"Whatever you say. How about another shot?" He waves to the bartender at the other end.

IT HAS BEEN three hours since Garret arrived at Matty's. Since then Angela and Avery have also arrived and the bar has been filled to the brim locals and farm hands. We have a table in the back corner that is filled with our empty bottles and our coats grace the back of the chairs. Every so often we take a break from dancing and sit to rest our feet while throwing back more shots and adding songs to the playlist on TouchTunes.

The first notes of Shania pump through the speakers and all three of us stand and rush to the dance floor. Garret sits alone at the table messing with his phone. He has made a few passes at Avery tonight which has thrown me off, but maybe I am just drunk and wishful thinking is taking over. Avery would be great for him, and an awesome sister in law for me. I can't help but wonder what she thinks about my twin.

"So, Ave, uhhh…." A giggle comes out of me paired with a snort. "What are your intentions with my brother?" Beer flies out of Angela's mouth as Avery immediately stops dancing and her demeanor instantly changes.

"Uhhhh." Her body is fidgety. "I need a shot. Yeah! Let's get a shot." Her words are rushed and she is nervous as hell when she takes off to the bar. "Joni, another round of shots please?"

"Avery, what the fuck?"

"Why are you asking me that? What did he tell you? Oh shit, does Zach know?"

I am completely drunk, but is she telling me that there really is something going on with her and Garret. Is this why he is home so much quicker than he normally would be? "I was just giving you shit, but now, now you spill."

"Oh it is nothing." She turns away

"I don't think hooking up in the hot tub at the B&B is nothing." Angela smirks. Now it is my turn to spit my beer out.

"You fucked my brother?" My voice is raised in shock and the song ends at the same time. Garret is across the bar so I doubt he heard me, but the people around for sure got a little peek into Avery and his sex life. She waves to Joni requesting more shots.

"Maybe we should talk about this tomorrow, when there isn't as much alcohol involved, when your brother isn't over there." She points her thumb behind her to exaggerate his close proximity. "It was a one time thing. He doesn't want more than that." Sadness fills her eyes and I get it. I get loving someone so much it hurts, then breaking more because they don't want you the same way, but she is wrong. Garret adores her and every time he sees her he loses his ability to function like a grown ass man. She thinks he is here for me, and it may have started that way, but he stayed for her. I will just have to prove it to her.

Fourteen

ZACH

The beeping tone on my phone pulls me away from the ledgers I am going over on my desk. I notice the stupid name that Garret saved his number under and chuckle.

G-Man: She's here at Matty's. Dancing with some farm hands.

Me: Dude. You either have to tell her you want more or be okay with her getting it somewhere else.

G-Man: Dick. What kind of best friend doesn't take my side?

Me: The kind that is trying to save you from the same fucked up situation that I am in,

G-Man: She is here too. Also dancing with some farm hands.

Me: MY FARM HANDS?

G-Man: Didn't you tell them to keep their distance. Man they aren't listening to you boss. 🤣

Me: That shit aint funny Garret. How bad is it?

THE PICTURE on my phone is of the table covered in empty beer bottles and stacks of disposable shot glasses. Based on the amount of time that Danni has been gone and the coats on the chairs, only four of them are drinking all of that. She is shit faced and blowing off steam. I have seen this before, she comes home, goes out, and does anything to make me jealous. Even if I am not there to see it she is dancing with my farm hands on purpose. She knows they guys will talk about it tomorrow, though they'd be stupid to.

My gut is telling me to keep my ass at home, but I am pissed at her and the dumbasses who didn't listen when I said she was off limits. It is late and Carter is asleep, he won't wake up for another couple hours to eat so I go to find Aunt Celia. She is in the living room cuddled up under a blanket on the couch, her newest book in her hands. What is it with women and these romance novels; us real men will never have a chance at living up to their book boyfriend and their innate ability to be perfect.

"Garret is at Matty's. He needs some help getting the girls home."

"Enjoy yourself a bit before you come back. I can take care of the baby, gives me an excuse to keep reading and not go to bed yet."

"It isn't like that Auntie. I told you I am respecting her boundaries."

"Whatever you say dear." She waves a hand to shoo me away and then turns the page in her book.

Matty's was built in an old building on the edge of town. To those passing by it might look like a dilapidated building if you turned off the neons. The land and building are something I acquired about 3 years ago when I bought the Matthew's farm. I didn't add the business to my catalog though, I want nothing to do with the bar. Joni has run the place for over twenty years, and I won't take that from her, plus the town needs a place to blow off steam. I do however help her with the finances and upkeep, so keeping up on the books is in my nature.

When I pull in, the makeshift parking lot is packed, and full of muddy holes. It reminds me that I need to get some gravel down before winter hits. I want to stay out of sight so I head to the back entrance. I can hear the music before I ever enter the bar, it is a slow song and I imagine that means they are at the table drinking, or at least I hope. I don't want to see her slow dancing with some other guy. It just hits different, it's more intimate. Instead of rushing out front I wait until the song ends and the mood is toward partying again.

I notice Garret first, sitting backwards in a chair, beer in hand, eyes glued on Avery. I'd be willing to bet big money there is drool on his chin right now and I haven't even looked at the group of girls yet. I make it to the table in a few steps, place my hand on his shoulder, and look in the same direction he is.

The entire bar blurs around Danni. She is wearing a come fuck me green dress that hugs her curves perfectly, stopping just low enough to keep people looking for a glimpse of what is above the hem. Her thigh high boots that guide my eyes straight to the place I want to devour. I'm fucked. My cock twitches and I try to remind myself that she is no longer mine. Garret pulls me out of my trance by handing me a beer and giving me a nod that says he understands. Garret has always approved of his sister and I's relationship, just not the way I fucked it up. He even feels a bit of responsibility because of his slip of information, though I would never blame him. The song ends and another starts to play, Danni moves from just dancing with Avery and Angela to one of the guys on the dance floor. Her right hand runs through her dark hair, holding it back off of her face while the other traces across the guy's shoulders before she turns around and shoves her ass into his waist. They find a rhythm to the song and when he starts to move his hand from her stomach to her inner thigh I stand. I pace to the bar for something stronger than the beer, making sure I hit her line of sight. When she notices me she stiffens, but I can't tell if it is because she sees me or because my farm hand fears for his job and steps away. Her eyes hold mine, and she licks her lips before trapping the bottom one between her teeth. Is she fucking teasing me, I almost liked it better when she tried to make me jealous. At least then she was making a point instead of giving me false hope. She breaks our gaze and walks to the girls whispering something in their ear.

I am standing at the bar waiting on Joni to take my order when I feel her hand on my shoulder. When I turn she has her coat on and her purse in hand. "Garret is going to make sure the girls get home. Can you get me to the cabin?" Her words are slurred and her grip on my arm is keeping her balanced.

"You want to go now? I thought it was girls' night?" I came to help Garret and let my presence be known to my employees, not to ruin her night. I don't want to fuck up my chances of her staying here. "I can go if that is it. I don't want to stop your fun."

"Eh, it isn't the same. It wasn't their hands I wanted on my body."

You know the saying ***drunk people speak the truth***, Lord let it be true. Not that I would do anything about it tonight, but maybe just maybe she still wants me too. "I see." My throat thickens, unsure what she expects from me, or if she can tell my cock is strained against my jeans. "I'll give you a ride."

Before heading home I stop by the 24 hour diner to grab her a burger. She needs something to soak up the alcohol and greasy food does the trick. The entire ride home Danni is fumbling with her damn boots. I have to hold in my laughs at her struggles, but also my urges when she exposes herself in different positions while trying to take them off. After enough entertainment for the night I offer her help.

"Here" I pat the center console instructing her to put her legs up there. When she does I use my right hand to unzip the boots, catching my breath as my fingers graze her inner thigh. It has been years since I have had the privilege to touch her there. My mouth waters as I imagine my lips pressing soft kisses in a path to her sweet pussy. I'd give anything to taste it again.

"Thanks" Her voice is a whisper, but full of something I can't determine. This dance we are doing is dangerous but I can't help myself.

"Always." I leave off part of the phrase that I have used our entire lives to tell her I love her. It isn't like I don't want to say it, but I know she doesn't want me to. So "always" will let her know that I am here for her whenever, and the silent "as" that came before it reminds me that I broke her heart and don't deserve her.

We pull up to the cabin and I tell her to wait in the truck. I run into the house to grab her some sandals so she doesn't have to walk on the cold muddy ground. I open the door and have her turn towards me to put the sandals on her feet, but she ignores me and jumps at me. Her arms wrap around my neck and I stumble backwards from surprise. I reach my arms around her to keep her from falling and my hands land on her ass as she wraps her legs around me. Her sweet aroma surrounds me adding to the discomfort in my pants, but the smell of beer and cinnamon remind me that she's drunk and none of this is real.

Once in the house I go to put her down, but her grip tightens. "It's been 3 years." She mumbles into my neck. "Three long years since I have felt the hands of a man bring me pleasure. Three long years filled with self fulfillment."

An internal war begins, I want to fulfill her needs, but I am pissed that it has only been three years. That means that some other man brought her pleasure. How can I have expected her to not have sex, to live a celibate life in which she climaxed only from her hands and toys. Fuck, I'm an asshole.

"Danni.."

She cuts me off pulling up to look in my eyes, "I need sex. I need to come from something other than my own hands"

"I.. ugh… you're drunk. Remember you hate me." I need to try anything to salvage this night, I can't give her a reason to leave.

"Fine! I'll do it myself." She slides off of me hiking her skirt in the process, but she doesn't notice. I do though, I notice her ass on display and the thin piece of black lace between that covers the space between the two plump rounds. My dumb ass follows her up the stairs.

"Listen D. You know it isn't like that. You told me this was a business relationship and I am trying to be on my best behavior. Carter needs you here and if I fuck this up then you will leave. I don't want to say I told you so in the morning."

"Damnit Zach, I am horny. I want a good hard fuck and if I remember correctly you used to do that to me. I'm not trying to fix our past, I just don't want to deal with finding a guy at the bar and having to ghost him for him to get the point it was just an itch I needed scratching. Nothing more." She pulls her dress over her head as she walks into the bedroom. Her matching lace bra and thong come off on her journey to the bed as she turns to face me. "You either want to help or not. It's up to you"

I grip the door frame above my head, forcing myself not to step into the room, but fuck I'd be lying if I tell her I don't want to help. She climbs onto the bed and spreads her legs providing me a view that nearly breaks me.

"You're running out of time. If I make myself come, you don't get to. Remember the nights you would make it happen over and over again." She is fucking with my head, this is a test and I can't give in. She moves her hand to her mouth sucking on her fingers before placing them between her folds. "I'm not much of a porn gal. I like to come to memories. Ones that happened long ago, say more than six years." Six years ago I was the one making her moan. She was screaming my name.

"There was this one time where I decided that I wanted to spend the weekend completely naked. I didn't leave the house for three days. My man left for work early in the morning and I wanted to surprise him. I did the laundry naked, the dishes, I even cooked naked." A growl escapes me, as the images of our weekend pop into my mind. I need to leave, but it feels like my feet are glued to the ground. She continues to tell the story while she rubs her clit, but she hasn't pressed inside herself yet. She's building up her story and playing me at the same time.

"It was about dinner time when he came home. I had on his favorite pair of my high heels, and was pulling the casserole out of the oven when he walked into the kitchen. My ass was on display for him and drew him in without words." She's right, it was fucking hot, but it is even hotter that she is pleasuring herself to the same memory. A moan escapes her lips while she uses her other hand to knead her breast and I'm about to come just watching her.

"That casserole stayed on top of the stove. I however ended up sprawled across the dining room table as his feast. I came over and over again that night, from his fingers, his tongue, his cock. He is definitely the best fuck I have ever had. I wonder what he is doing now?" For being drunk she sure is aware of what she is doing. It makes me wonder if she is more aware than she wants me to believe, so if I do give in she will have an excuse. Every word that comes out of her mouth decreases my ability to stay out of the room, every time she hitches her breath or moans I grip the frame tighter. That is until my name comes off her lips.

Fifteen

DANNI

I don't know what came over me in the bar that made me throw everything I had worked for in getting over Zach out the window. Actually I do. I haven't had sex in three years and damnit if his jealousy of another man's hands on me didn't turn me on.. He doesn't know I saw him, but when I turned to check on Garret he was there, then the next thing I knew he was walking through the dance floor to the bar. I was getting to him, and I wasn't even trying this time. So my heart went dumb and my libido started taking over. Zach was safe, well as safe as could be. He wouldn't hurt me or carry diseases. That is why I have been trying to tempt him since we got in the damn truck.

After a slow build up I finally break him by moaning his name just off of memories. He finally lets go of the door frame and takes his belt off as he is walking towards me. This whole time I have been in control, but something has changed. His deep voice hypnotizes me, "Be careful what you wish for baby."

Fuck, what was I thinking. Can I really have sex with Zach and let it just be sex? I have already started something I can't walk away from, and my heart is in for a beating, I just hope the one my pussy takes is worth it.

He grabs my hands and ties them to the headboard with his belt. "If it's an orgasm you're after, I'll give it to you." He is demanding as he places his hands on my ankles and rubs them up my calves and towards my inner thighs. His desire takes over when he gets to where my hips meet my core and he swipes his thumb over my folds. "Damn baby, you're so fucking wet. All this on a memory of me tasting you?"

"Mmhmm"

"Let me make that memory a reality then." He leans in and his tongue drags across my clit. He nibbles and sucks and I may come right now. "Is this what you wanted, baby?"

"Yes, fuck yes!"

"What else do you want D?"

I don't know how to answer that question. A typical one night stand would have been some vanilla sex. Not knowing someone makes it hard to ask for things you truly like, but Zach and I were never vanilla. Even when we first started having sex we always were out of the box. I waited too long because the next thing I know Zach has two thick fingers inside my pussy, and if I thought I would go before this is more intense. I hear him growl in pleasure as I buck towards his face and wish I could fist his hair, but the damn belt has me constrained. One word is all it takes to move on. "More"

Zach looks up at me and winks, then he is right back to nibbling on the bundle of nerves between my legs but his fingers slow as he massages my back side with his pinkie. It is exactly what I want, the orgasms this way are phenomenal, but he was the last one to play with my ass, even I don't do that. When he inserts his finger I explode, my legs clench around his head and his name escapes again.

"Mhmmm you taste so sweet, even better than I remember." He moves his fingers to my mouth and I open to suck my juices from him. I want so much more, I need so much more. He leaves my hands tied to the headboard and moves to the en suite bathroom. I hear the water running, is he pleasuring himself while I am strapped to this damn bed? What the actual fuck?

Within minutes he walks back into the bedroom, clearly not relieved, but unbuckles the belt. "The bath is filling up, rose water is already in it. I'll make you some tea, go relax." Then he leaves, he just fucking leaves. I am too stunned to stop him, he doesn't seem pissed. There is a sorrow in his eyes, a weight in his shoulders, it is as if he is in pain.

The water is hot and soothes the aches in my body, but not in my heart. I already regret what happened tonight and I haven't even had the night to sleep on it. I don't know why I ever thought that I could sleep with Zach and it ever be just sex. Tears well in my eyes as I try to force away the emotions, but one escapes and falls down my cheek as Zach enters with a mug of hot tea. I try to wipe it away before he sees it but I am not quick enough.

"I'm sorry Danni. I never should have given in to you. You had been drinking and I knew better. I knew you didn't really want me, and I hurt you again. Please just please don't give up on the farm because of this. Carter needs you here and I will do whatever it takes, just tell me what it is."

I can't look at him. It feels good to hear him apologize for hurting me, but he shouldn't. I knew exactly what I was doing and I wanted it, probably more than him. I wanted more and he had the strength to stop. If I look at him I will spill it all, that I still love him, that I need him, that I don't hate him. I'll tell him it was just easier to hate him than to be heart broken, and then I will fall in love again, just for him to walk away again when it gets too much. Eventually he leaves the bathroom.

When I wake up the next morning Zach isn't in the cabin, which means he didn't sleep here. I am not surprised since Carter was in the main house with Aunt Celia. I'm a little relieved that I don't have to face him first thing this morning, but I still want to know more.

I have been staring at the safe for thirty minutes, sipping on my tea, trying to decide if I really want to know what the letters say. Are they even real? I'm a coward and haven't even opened the safe yet.

"Here goes nothing." I enter my birthdate into the safe. Typical Zach, predictable and stuck in his ways, the safe beeps and opens. In it is a wooden box that has been hand decorated with burning. Running horses grace the lid and dogwoods surround the sides. Between two trees on the front, my name is scribed., When I open it I see a pile of envelopes, at least fifty. Beside the letters sits a velvet box, one I don't have to open to know what is inside. I can still picture the day he put it on my finger, and worse the day I took it off.

There is a heaviness in my chest and fear of what is written on those papers overwhelms me. I don't know if I can stomach why he chose someone else over me. What I can do is ride, clear my head and embrace the open land. Kash is what I need right now.

I close the box and place it back into the safe before changing into warmer clothes. Now that I have actually unpacked and my clothes aren't shoved in a suitcase that sits upon the leather loveseat in my bedroom, it takes me less time to change and I arrive at the barn within twenty minutes.

Sixteen

DANNI

Angela looks up from her decorating as the bell rings when I open the door to the bakery. It doesn't get past me that her smile is a little bigger today with Carter in my arms then when she normally sees me. Last night she came to the cabin and I told her everything over a few bottles of wine and popcorn. Everything about Carter that is, I left out the part about sleeping with his dad. I was exhausted from the night before with Zach, but I needed her to know. I needed someone who was on my team first, not Zach's, but was also bold enough to tell me the truth without holding back. She understands the pain I have been caused but is also elated that I get to be a mom. She squeals, dropping the piping bag on the counter and rushes towards me with open arms.

"The only thing that could make this shop any sweeter, Baby C." She assesses me to see if I am going to let her take him or if I am still latched on with the newness of my discovery.

"Oh, take him." I laugh "I want to try the strawberry macarons anyways!" I step behind the counter and grab a couple. Angela never used to carry them, they are expensive to make and not really that popular in such a rural area, but when I tried them on one of our trips to Italy and couldn't stop talking about them she was determined to perfect them. She makes sure to have the strawberry and orange flavors anytime I am in town. I bite into one and melt, "Mmm! These are better than Italy."

"They should be, I have spent years making them Danni approved!"

"I'm glad I didn't order these for tonight, the others wouldn't get any." I laugh as I take another bite of the cookie.

"I have your cheesecake in back, but I also have a box of macarons for you too. I tried some new flavors and would like your opinion."

"You are the best. I haven't truly seen Lilly in ages so it will be nice to have them for dinner, cheesecake is her favorite. I haven't made a family dinner since I've left. Everything is go, go, go and even when I visit mom and dad it isn't like it used to be."

"It seems like you are settling back into Missouri life just fine." The raised eyebrow and glare tells me it is more of a question than a statement.

I know that there are so many reasons to pick Zach's farm for the study. The number one being that it is the best application and will yield the most valuable data, this is also home and Angela, Aunt Celia, and my son are all here. I just don't know if I can take it. I stare out the window contemplating all the outcomes of choosing Turner Farms or not choosing Turner Farms.

"Hey, D, everything will be okay." She touches my arm softly. "Choosing the farm doesn't mean choosing him. They aren't one in the same. Also, not choosing the farm doesn't mean giving up Carter." I know she is right, but what if I want it to be the same thing?

"I know it is just a lot to choose in such a limited time. My heart still hurts and now I am connected to the man who causes it for life." A weight hits my shoulders, but a coo from Carter catches my attention and I am instantly drawn out of my funk. The bell rings above the door and I take Carter back from Angela so she can wait on the incoming customer.

She catches her breath as soon as she turns and sees the customer. He isn't a local and I can't tell if she has met him before, but the look on her face says she is excited to see him now. After a few minutes I can tell this is their first encounter. The way she is stumbling over her words is something I have never seen. She is lost in his ocean blue eyes and I am pretty sure she would reach out and run her hands through his dark curls if she could. If it were 10 years ago she would have, but heartbreak has changed her confidence over the years. Truth be told it was that cheating asshole of an ex husband, Tyler, who did it.

Tyler was a financial analyst that Angela met on one of our trips. We were staying at a resort in Tahiti five years ago, inspired by one too many bottles of wine we decided to crash a wedding on the beach. Tyler was the best man, which is not an accurate description at all. She fell head over heels, they dated for six months long distance and then eloped. He moved in with her after they wed, stating that he traveled a lot and it didn't matter where he was based out of, but kept his apartment in New York for the convenience of traveling there for "monthly meetings." Angela joined him once a month to the big apple early in the marriage but after about six months Tyler would convince her that he'd be in the office late and she'd be bored and alone. On their first anniversary she flew to surprise him, when she walked in she saw Tyler thrusting into a brunette bent over the side of the couch. She has been broken since, feeling unworthy of love.

"I'm sorry I don't have any kringles, but I hope you enjoy the creme puff."

"I'm sure it will be delicious. Just a bit homesick is all, and thought a kringle might help."

The man turns to leave, but as he reaches the door Angela finally gets a bit of her confidence back. She is standing straighter when she says, "Sir, come back tomorrow and I'll be sure to have a kringle with your name on it." He smiles and her confidence fades, as she trips over her words. "I mean, not actually on it, but it will be yours."

"Thank you, but you don't have to."

"I can't promise it will be like your grandma's but I'll try." The man nods his head and leaves. Angela runs to the door and watches him walk to the car. Once he drives away she squeals jumping up and down like a young school girl.

"Girl, sleeping baby!" I whisper-yell and laugh.

"Did you see that man! He has the body of a Greek god and his eyes, lord have mercy, his eyes." She fans herself with both hands as she plops down into the chair across from me.

"I haven't seen you act like that since Tyler, even on the beaches full of gorgeous men."

"He is different, I don't know what it is, but between him standing in front of me and Carter being in the same room, my ovaries are melting." She giggles.

"Well go cool off in the walk in and grab my cheesecake. I have to get home and start cooking.

After unloading the cheesecake and laying Carter down in the nursery, I start making noodles. The recipe is simple, but it is the one meal I associate with home. Grama used to make them, then dad, now me, maybe Carter will make them one day too. The eight pounds of noodles drying on the countertop should be enough to feed everyone and send them home with leftovers.

There isn't much I can do between now and starting the chicken, and with Carter asleep I can't go back to the cabin, so I spread the files of the top four candidates for the grant across the desk in Zach's office. There isn't really a choice here, I know the best farm for the study, I just don't know if I am ready to commit. I move the file for Turner Farms to the side and narrow down the top three to find a runner up, seeing if it will be enough to not stay in Missouri. I critique every application against the same standards and checklist until I have my answer, Sander's Dairy Farm in a small town in Idaho. It would be the obvious choice if Turner Farm's didn't enter an application. Unfortunately for Mr. Sanders, they did.

Normally I would call the first choice and offer them the grant first, just in case they changed their mind and I would need to go with another. However, there is no way Zach is turning this down. Mr. Sanders answers on the first ring. The conversation is short. I thank him for his interest in the program, but let him know that we have gone with another farm. I also let him know that he was in our top four applicants so he will be getting a free download of one of our systems already on the market and $3000.00. After I hang up I call the other 2 farms. By the time I am done contacting the other farms I am ready to start the chicken. I decide that tonight's dinner will be as good as any to let Zach know I have chosen Turner Farms, so I don't provide him with the usual congratulatory call.

An hour later I finished cooking dinner, set the large dining room table, and fed Carter. Aunt Celia is watching him while I clean the mess from cooking in the kitchen before I head to the Cabin to clean myself up as well. I step out onto the porch into the crisp November evening. The trees sway with the breeze as their gold and amber leaves begin to fall. Lilly and Andy will be here soon, so I hurry to the side by side and drive to the cabin. It doesn't take long until I am no longer covered in flour and my makeup is touched up. This is a casual dinner, no need for a fancy dress, so I pull on my go-to cozy outfit, leggings and Chiefs sweater and drive back to the house.

Lilly jumps out of the cab of Andy's truck and nearly tackles me when she sees me step out of the ATV. The last time I saw her was with Carl and she tried her hardest to make the meeting quick. Knowing what I know now, she didn't want me to catch on to Zach's plan and she isn't the best at secrets. Tonight she is one hundred percent herself, also sporting leggings and a yellow Kansas City hoodie hiding the baby bump. It may be Sunday dinner, but it is also week nine in the NFL and Kansas City has the Sunday Night game. Everyone here in our little town is unique, but they share a few opinions; support locals, no one bakes better than Angela, and football is only second to farming in our blood, especially the Kansas City Chiefs.

"Oh my god! Danni you look amazing! I am so glad you are home, and I am even happier I don't have to keep a secret from you any more." He words are filled with excitement and she kisses my cheek.

"I missed you too Lilly." I hook my arm through hers, "How about dinner, I had Angela whip up your favorite dessert."

"Cheesecake?" Her eyes go wide with anticipation.

"Damn, I thought it was a German Chocolate Cake." I snicker knowing full well she hates coconut.

She shoves me lightly, playing along "How could you forget something so important?"

"I guess that is what happens when someone tries to trick me. Come on I made Grama's chicken and noodles."

We make our way into the house and find Andy and Zach playing with Carter. Two gruff farm fellas cooing like babies, letting their soft centers show. Lilly leans up and whispers in my ear, "They are like M&Ms, hard on the outside and soft in the center." She leaves me giggling as she makes her way towards my son. I follow suit longing to be near both Carter and Zach, needing to feel at home.

Eventually we make our way to the dining room where we sit around the large oak table. It is tradition at the Turner's that no one sits at the head of the table, or opposite it. They are reserved to honor those who came before us, giving them a spot in our current lives, showing appreciation for their contributions to the family farm. Zach's grandpa said that his dad started the tradition when his parents died. They started the farm and they deserved to be a part of it forever.

"Damn Danni! This is delicious." Zach says as he layers potatoes onto his roll, then noodles on the potatoes and shoves it in his mouth.

"Did you forget that I can cook?" I laugh, sass evident.

"Nope! He just hasn't eaten anything as good since you left." Lilly pauses with fear in her eyes when she realizes what she said.

"It is absolutely amazing." Andy jumps in to save his wife as she silently mouths sorry.

"Actually…" I turn my body to face Zach who is sitting on my left. "I was wondering if you would be interested in letting me stay in the cabin for a bit longer. I know the situation isn't the best but I would really like to spend as much time with Carter as possible and it will cut down on driving time. Also, it will make it easier for both of us to see him everyday and not shuffle him to the B&B. The B&B isn't really baby friendly. I understand if you aren't comfortable with it, so I could look for a house in town to rent."

"Danni, the cabin belongs to you. It always has."

"I appreciate that, but I also know you stay there sometimes. So I was thinking that maybe it would be best for Carter if we both stayed there, you can have the master and I can stay in one of the other rooms. Carter needs both of his parents, Zach."

"Ummm..." His hands grip the back of his neck and his jaw clenches as he contemplates what to say next.

Maybe I was wrong, maybe he did change his mind after last night and he doesn't want me here, why is he delaying his answer. I knew last night screwed things up for us. I tempted him and now he doesn't want me around. How stupid could I possibly be? There is no way that we are going to be able to live under the same room if this is how he feels after last night.

"Don't worry about it, I will get a house. We can discuss the arrangements with Carter at a different time. The study pays for my living expenses anyways." I feel the tears forming and I excuse myself from the table before they fall.

Seventeen

ZACH

I don't know what the fuck just happened. We are all there sitting around the table thanking Danni for cooking and telling her how delicious the food is. Then Danni asks if she can live in the cabin, if I will move in there with her. My mind turned to mush and I didn't know how to answer her. I don't know if this is her way of telling me she picked the farm, or if she is giving up on her dreams again. I also don't know if last night has something to do with it. I just wanted her to pick the farm first, not because she felt like she had to. When she excuses herself from the dining room I see the glistening of tears in her eyes.

The dining room is silent and all eyes are stuck on me. No one is talking. Lilly isn't even moving towards the cheesecake. I nod my head at them and scoot my chair back, breaking the silence when the legs scrape across the hardwood. I don't know how to explain to Danni why I stumbled, that her reasoning determines my answer, but I grab a blanket on my way out to the porch.

Danni is sitting on the step leaning against the rail, she is folded in on herself trying to fight the tears and defend herself from the cold wind. I wrap the blanket around her before sitting beside her. She doesn't speak, she just continues to stare out into the farm with quiet sobs escaping her.

"I need to know why." My tone is quiet, kind, but it hits her hard as her sobs begin to quicken and her shoulders shake. "I need to know if it is because you are doing the study here, or because you are giving up on your dreams again without telling me." The last point has her turn towards me, and the pain in her face stabs me right in the heart.

"Again?"

I have never told her the truth about breaking off the wedding, about Garret letting it slip about the job offer. "Washington, you were going to turn it down and you didn't even tell me they offered it to you."

"I didn't want it." She tries to sound confident and sure of her words, but I know her better.

"Bullshit. Don't try that with me. You worked your ass off, it was everything you wanted and you were just going to throw it all away without speaking to me. We were getting married and you didn't even let me in on the choice." I'm angry now. For the first time in my life I am realizing it wasn't just about her dream. It was that she made a life choice without me, even though we had made so many together, she shut me out on this one. "If you didn't want it you would have told me about it. You wanted it, honey, and you deserved it."

"Not as bad as I wanted you!" Her words hits me like whiplash. I clearly made her feel like she had to make a choice, me or her dreams. I always tried to make sure that she knew I supported her, that I would do anything to make her happy, yet somewhere along the line I failed her and made her think she couldn't be with me and follow her dreams.

"I couldn't let you give everything up just for me." I'm not sure if she will believe the next words that come out of my mouth so I contemplate if I should even say them. "I would have gone with you, had you told me. We could have moved together, made a life there."

She is silent, shit, I knew she wouldn't believe me. It's true though. I would have given anything to make her happy.

I gave up everything to make her happy.

She was my home and it didn't have to be on this farm. My dad would have been pissed, it would have taken some getting used to, not working on the family farm, but someone else's as a hand. But I would have done it for her, she never gave me the chance, just like I never gave her the chance to stay.

"I couldn't ask you to go. I know your heart was always here, so I chose to stay. I chose you Zach."

"I chose you too, Danni. I chose to sacrifice my happiness, my dreams to let you live yours. I hate it. I hate waking up everyday knowing that I let the love of my life walk away, no, I pushed the love of my life away, it kills me. Then I see all the great things you are doing, earning awards and shit, and I know that I may be a miserable nobody, but my choice made you happy. You hate me and I get it. I fucked up, then I made it worse by acting like it was because I didn't love you enough, but I didn't do it to sleep around D. I did it for you."

"It wasn't just your choice! You may think you did something right, but you made me carry around the weight of hating you for years. You made me not want to be in my hometown, you made me so broken that I made it my personal vendetta to piss you off. Fuck the awards, the apps, the studies, I am married to my job and am a horrible person.

I have built bad habits of shutting people out because the one person I loved broke me. How can I be a good mom if this is who I am?"

She breaks, I wrap my arms around her unsure if it will make it worse, but at this point she needs someone to relieve some of the pain. I did this and I know that I have to figure out a way to fix it.

"Carter is lucky to have you D. We can figure out our mess, and still be good parents."

After a few minutes of sobbing, her body begins to relax. "I chose the farm. I didn't do it because of Carter. It was the right choice for the study, but I promise it wasn't for Carter."

"Even if it was D, I would be the last person to throw it in your face. Shit you were probably less likely to pick Turner because of me than you were to pick it because of Carter." A sense of relief fills me knowing she isn't giving up on her dreams. "We will make the cabin work, but you get the master. I haven't slept in it since the day you left. I can't. It just reminds me of what I lost."

She stands, "We should get back inside. I am cold and want cheesecake." The surprise on her face gives me hope but her immediate need to leave me reminds me that she is here for two things, the study and Carter. Last night was a mistake in her eyes and now I have lost all hope that I can win her love back.

It is the third quarter and Kansas City is up by 3. It is a good game and after a few beers Danni is at least enjoying her time with Lilly. I however am trying to figure out how I am going to live under the same roof as her for two years and not go crazy.

"A penny for your thoughts." Andy leans against the wooden beam in between the kitchen and living room.

"I don't know if I can do this."

"It's a little late now, Boss. She picked the farm, you have Carter. There is no turning back."

"Yeah. I guess so." It isn't like I want to turn back. Having Danni here is a best case scenario at least for Carter. He gets to be in the same place as both of his parents, co parenting as a team instead of being shuffled from place to place every other weekend. Me on the other hand, I went from leaving town to avoid her and the heartbreak that comes with her presence to living under the same damn roof.

The girls jump up screaming as our quarterback connects with the tight end for another touchdown. They start to giggle as they sush each other reminding themselves that Carter is asleep upstairs. Lilly rushes to Andy, to talk about the play, Danni turns watching her friend snuggle into her husband. Her eyes meet mine, a small smile graces her face and she tips her beer to me. I return the motion before I take the final swig of the bottle, I am thankful for the excuse to break the connection and get another beer.

By the end of the game Lilly is to the point of exhaustion that she needs Andy to help her to the truck. We are all hoping the baby will be here before the new year. Danni on the other hand, drank enough for her and the pregnant Lilly, so I help her up the stairs to the guest room before cleaning up the living room. After I pack the snacks away and toss the beer bottles I find my way to my room as well. Normally I can fall asleep quickly, tonight hundreds of scenarios are running through my mind. The worst one follows me into sleep and I dream of Danni. In my dream she meets some guy, falls in love, and moves far away with my son. I lose them both before I wake up sweating, thirsty, and pissed.

Eighteen

DANNI

I have reread the same paragraph four times, trying to get myself out of my head and into the story, but it just isn't working. Usually a hot cup of tea and my latest romance book helps, but right now all I can think about is the way Zach's fingers felt inside me as his tongue brushed my sensitive area. It is the first time I have felt like that since I moved. I haven't been in a real relationship since then, the closest was three months of vanilla sex and no connection with a guy in Birmingham. As much as I don't want to admit it, last night was more than pleasure, the connection was still there. I was stupid to think that I could just mess around with him and it would not impact my heart, especially after his confession last night.

I lean back in my chair, close my eyes and picture Zach's face between my thighs. My hand drifts slowly up my inner thigh grazing all the places I imagine him kissing, slowly making its way to my core. I can feel my wetness through my anties, and my nipples harden under my silk tank top. Before I can swipe my fingers under the seam I am startled by a clearing throat.

"Shit Zach, how long have you been standing there?"

A smirk crosses his face, "Long enough to hear you whisper my name while you teased yourself."

"I did not!" Did I? Was I saying things out loud without realizing it? Certainly he is fucking with me.

"Oh you did sweetheart." He closes the distance between us, but I am too stunned to sit up, or even close my legs. His eyes trace the form of my body and back up until he meets mine again. "If you are going to moan my name, I should at least get to be the one making you do it."

That does it, he wants to play dirty so can I. I stand and walk to the refrigerator needing to have my back to him when I speak. I refuse to let him see my face and question my confidence. "Oh, Zach, don't you see, you were the one making me do it. I was imagining your tongue and fingers in place of my hands. I'd say it was even better than the real thing." I sneak a peak over my shoulder with the last sentence.

"Ouch, how so?" He steps back clinching his heart as if hit by an imaginary bullet.

I grab a yogurt and turn with an evil grin, "The only mess it makes is when I come." I go to walk past him but he traps me between his beautifully sculpted arms. His throat bobs as he contemplates what he is going to say, but his eyes stare as if he can read my thoughts through mine. He leans in close and flicks my ear with his tongue, then whispers "Liar." If I wasn't wet before I am now. He pushes off the refrigerator and turns to pour him a cup of tea like nothing just happened.

"Obviously you can stay in the cabin, like I said last

night, it is yours. I agree that Carter needs us both and it isn't fair to make you do all the nightly duties so I will move into one of the other rooms." His voice is calm, matter of fact, businesslike. "But we need to set some ground rules."

Obviously we need rules. Co-parenting isn't the easiest thing in the world, scheduling, feedings, diapers, all need to be worked out. "Sure, obviously your work hours are pretty regular and I can adjust mine some. We can take turns with all things Carter, I can make a schedule." I leave out anything that would be about us messing around. This little cat and mouse game is fun, but we both play it and know there is a line we almost crossed and can't get there again.

"That isn't what I mean. I mean with you and me."

"Oh.." Exactly what I wanted. He has to be the first one to say there is something out loud, put it on him and keep your cards hidden Danni.

"However you seek pleasure is your business."

"I agree"

"You can't be a dick tease Danni! You can't just be camped in the kitchen making yourself come moaning my name and expect me to just be okay."

"Would you rather I moan someone else's?" I know I am pushing his buttons, but fuck I am wet and horny and he is the reason for it. A little payback never hurt anyone. "I'm sure it isn't my face you're picturing when your fucking your hand. Tell me Zach, which local whore are you moaning to."

He stalks into his bedroom but returns within minutes with something in his hand. He slides it across the countertop to me and runs his hands through his hair. I see my writing on the front cover and my heart stops.

To the love of my life:

Inside this case you will find your dreams have come true. My body was made for you to worship and damn do you worship it. I know you will enjoy this as a reminder of home when you are away.

Love Your Wife,
Dannielle Turner

I PICK up the case to open it and find the three discs that I had placed inside. Each one with a hand written note.

Disc 1: This one wasn't as fun to make. You weren't there. Enjoy the photos.

Disc 2: There is no way you forgot the way I fell during the spin on the pole. See me through your eyes.

Disc 3: No need to remember Cozumel, you can watch it over and over.

I DON'T KNOW if I am pissed or flattered. For six years this man has used me as his personal pornography library. The first disc is host to a set of photos that range from sexy boudoir to playboy spread. The second is a strip tease and lap dance I did for him in a personal room in Vegas. I had both phones set at different angles to record and then edited it for his pleasure. The final disc is a video of us. I made our suite in Cozumel a studio and captured every bit of sex we had that week. There was so much content it could be a full length feature film.

I gave this to him as an early wedding gift on the night of his bachelor party. I didn't even know he opened it, or why he would, considering he was the one that broke it off.

The tears falling on my cheeks catch me off guard. Am I hurt that he took something so intimate and held on to it when he didn't have the right, or is it because the front cover reminds me of what could have been? What should have been.

"You… you opened this?"

"Of course I did. It was a gift from you. I opened it on the way to the bar with the guys. When I read the descriptions I hid it in my coat pocket, so no one could see."

"But, you used it? You looked at those pictures, and watched the videos, even after you broke my heart." Unsure if I am strong enough to keep standing I find a way to a chair.

"Not at first. I was miserable. I didn't just break your heart Danni, I broke mine too. I wrote to you. I dialed your number but never called. I even flew to Washington once."

"Why?"

"Because I loved you, why else?"

"No, why did you start watching them?"

"Not for the reason you are thinking. I knew the Danni in those images and videos was happy. We were at our best, in love with a future. I hated what I had done to you and every time I wrote, almost called, or tried to get you back in any way I felt guilty. I hated that the last time I saw you, you weren't happy. So I watched them."

"But you did use them for other purposes?"

"About a year after you left I went on a trip with Garret. We were in Canada fishing and I met a girl at the hotel bar. She kept hitting on me and Garret was already upstairs with her friend. She was beautiful, and I was horny, but the thought of sleeping with someone else made me sick. I couldn't even watch porn without feeling like I was being the man I told you I wanted to be. I didn't want to make the lie the truth. So, I watched the second disc as soon as I got home."

There are too many things running through my head to try and speak. First and foremost, how could I have been so blind to see that something else had to be going on for Zach to end it? He had never given any inclination that he wasn't happy or wanted something different. Guilt fills me and I wonder if I made myself hate Zach because I didn't want to fight for us. That I wanted to blame him, when the truth was I wanted Washington and he gave me a way out. I was too much of a coward to see it, and now that I do, remorse takes form in the vile that rises in the back of my throat.

"I know you don't want to hear it, but Elizabeth was the only other person I slept with. I felt I owed it to her, to let her try and have a baby. After the first time I slept with her I vomited. Truth of the matter is, we did IVF because I couldn't sleep with her. It wasn't a struggle to get pregnant, it was a struggle to try. Danni we didn't even sleep in the same room."

It feels like hours that he stares at me, waiting for any sort of response. For the first time I am questioning my part in all of this and I can't respond without my typical over thinking of everything. If I say something right now in the moment of pain and shock I might regret it later. This situation we are in is fragile and it isn't just him and I anymore. My son, our son, he has to be the reason for all things. He is also my current savior when I hear him cry, an excuse to leave Zach and this topic of conversation.

Nineteen

ZACH

For the first time in six years I have hope. Hope that I didn't ruin the rest of my life. Hope that I can get Danni to stay here and I won't lose her and my son. Hope that if she stays I can fix any fuck up I have done in the past. I will do anything to turn that hope into a reality.

I spent the morning working over the numbers with Andy. I know that he and Lilly have big plans to grow their family, but he doesn't feel like he can do that if he isn't established on their own. He is already stressed about the baby that will be here within the month. I have been reflecting on what is important since Danni showed back up, and I realize that my mom would be disappointed in the way I have been focused on the farm and the money rather than the people.

CJ Farms is already set to stay under that name and will always be a separate entity of Turner Farms. Once Danni has completed her study on the farm I can execute my plan to keep Andy and Lilly close, I just hope two years isn't too long for them to wait. They have the house that they built on the east side of my farm. I gave them the land a few years ago, land that is sandwiched between my farm and the one I am purchased from Mr. Jensen.

"Listen Andy, I really appreciate everything you do for the farm. You're a good man."

"Just doing my job Boss."

"No, you're not. You do so much more. Thank you. For all of it."

"Boss, you know I love working for you, but Lilly and I have been talking."

"I know, you are ready to branch out on your own."

"Yes, sir."

"I understand that. Where ya looking at?"

"Well, sir, since you own so much of the land in the county, there isn't really anywhere close for us. I have been looking online. We have found a few places, some in central Kansas, the most promising though looks to be in Idaho."

I lean back in my chair, and run my hand across my chin. I want to give him the farm, but I can't take the chance of Danni leaving. Not now, when Carter just got her.

"I see. You and Lilly are important to me, not just in the business, you're family."

"Yes, boss. We'd love to find something closer, but the economy just isn't making it easy on us."

"How soon are you thinking?"

"We're planning a trip this weekend to Idaho, might make an offer then."

"Keep me updated. Good luck Andy."

Andy shakes my hand and leaves the office. I am supposed to meet Garret at the garage to show him the Mustang, but I need to fix this situation with Andy and Lilly first.

Me: Can you meet me at the Bakery? I'll buy the coffee and dessert. I need to talk about the study.

Danni: Sure, what time?

Me: Sooner the better.

Danni: I am already in town. Be there in 15.

DANNI IS SITTING in the bakery by the time I get there. She already has a cup of hot tea and a plate with some new pastry on it that I haven't seen before. She is focused on her computer and doesn't notice me until I am already at the table. When her eyes meet mine I can tell she is in strictly business mode, which is great for me. I don't have time to get worked up with her here, and Angela would one hundred percent take her side. I don't need to be ganged up on.

"Um, what the fuck is that." I point to the pastry on the plate.

"Oh, that is the newest item added to the menu. It is called a Kringle. It is for Oliver."

"Who the hell is Oliver?"

"A new guy in town. Moved from Wisconsin, came in the other day wanting a kringle to cure his bout of homesickness.

Angela lost her shit, probably pissed herself in the process. It was so bad she stumbled over her words."

"Fuck."

"Right, so now I have to try every new batch she makes, and it doesn't matter how many times I tell her they are delicious, *it isn't as good as his grandmas!"* She rolls her eyes so hard that they might get stuck back there. I can't help but laugh, but steal a bite of the pastry anyways.

"Damn, it looks like shit, but it tastes phenomenal."

"She's in back, you should tell her."

Instead of getting up from the table I holler out. "Angela, a black coffee and one of these ugly ass pastries please." Danni chuckles and sips her tea as Angela comes running from the back.

"It is ugly isn't it." She comes around the corner wiping her hands on her apron. "He will never ask me out if I serve him this." Danni and I both laugh again while she pours my coffee. "He hasn't been back since that first day, and thank goodness, because I told him I'd have a Kringle and can't get it right."

I stand to kiss her cheek, "He'd be stupid not to. They are delicious." She thanks me and goes back to whatever she was working on in the back of the bakery.

"So, Oliver huh. You got a last name? I can check him out."

"It's cute that you think you can find out more about him than I can."

"I have my sources." I snicker

"I'm a tech genius, Zach. I don't need sources." Her smile hits her eyes, she is full of pride and it hits me that I may have done the right thing after all.

After an hour of discussing my intentions with CJ Farms, Danni and I have come up with a solution. I will keep a one percent stake in the entity so she can still do the study across all aspects of my farm and still be within the restraints of the grant. Andy and Lilly will receive all financial gains and technology resources after the study and I will purchase what is needed for my farm. After the study is over I will sell my one percent to Andy and Lilly for the same minute amount of money I am selling the other 99 percent to them for. One dollar.

After trying three more varieties of kringles to appease Angela I excuse myself from the bakery and head to the garage to meet Garret. Again I am the last one to my arranged meetings, if it was with anyone else it would piss me off.

Garret is leaning against his old Ford in his old blue jeans, a ball cap, and flannel jacket, a rare sight since he earned his wings. Even when he is home between flights he is wearing some fancy shit, not quite GQ model, but definitely not farm boy.

“What I am about to show you stays between you and me man. Don’t try and pull that “she’s my twin, I have to tell her” bullshit either. I am only telling you because I know you’d be pissed if I didn’t let you help.”

“Oh ho ho, you bought the damn car didn’t you? You really are trying to win her back.”

I punch his arm and he rubs the pain away but still chuckles, “well, let me see her.”

We walk into the old garage and I pull the tarp off of the Mustang. “I guess there is no point in trying to lie and tell you the car is for me then, huh?”

Garret walks around the car lightly grazing his hand across the body and whistles. “You promised her that you’d get her this car on our 16th birthday. You're full of shit if you thought that I would think you’d buy it for any other reason.”

"It needs some work, but I figure that between Danni and Avery you and I do too."

"You can say that again."

"What is your time off looking like in the near future?"

Garret grips his neck with one hand and taps his other on the hood. The twitch of his mouth says he has something to say but isn't quite ready. I stare at him raising my brows letting him know that I will wait all day for him to spill.

"I'm thinking of making some changes. Ones that will allow me to be home more often."

"Oh yeah? Like what man?"

"I bought a plane."

"I'm sorry you are over here giving me shit because I bought the woman I have loved since I was a kid her dream car, but you're out here buying planes for Avery."

"Whoa man, I didn't say it was for Avery."

"C'mon Garret, you think I don't know that being a pilot was your dream. The only way you'd ever give that up is for a girl."

"I'm not giving it up. I'm just changing pace. We are 32 years old, and I want a family. Living in the air isn't the way to make it happen."

"So what's the plan Casanova?"

"Well I still have mom and dad's house, so finding a place to stay won't be hard. I am going to find some land and build a strip. I am a qualified instructor so I will give flying lessons. I have a nice nest egg, it won't take much of it to get up and going."

"That's great, but I meant your plan with Avery. Have you told her yet?"

"I don't think she's interested man, we had our hookup, but she has never implied she wanted more. Don't women do that if that is what they want?"

"Fuck if I know man, I can't figure your sister out the last few days."

Over the next few hours we talk about the car, making a list of what we need and how we plan to keep it a secret from Danni. Garret is a shit liar, especially to her, so we plan times that she won't be asking to meet him for lunch or dinner. We make a deal that if she calls we stop and he does what she wants. We also plan to use his new adventure to our advantage, but we have to be careful. Danni will want to support her brother in any way and pop up visits to see the plane are bound to happen.

Garret shows me pictures of the plane and explains his plans to me. I don't think I have seen him more excited for anything in his life. He talks about how he will get to stay home, find a girl, and settle down. How his mom has been begging for grandkids and how she knows he is more likely to give them to her than Danni. That is when I text Danni and tell her Zach is coming to dinner, and that we need to tell him about his nephew.

Twenty

DANNI

My parents arrived this morning to meet their grandson, but the surprises keep on coming. At lunch today, Garret told us that his last flight is this weekend. I think my parents are sad that this means they won't see him as often since he won't be traveling, but they are still supportive of the changes he is making. I, however, am ecstatic that I will get to see him more, and that he will get to be a large part of Carter's life.

I don't know what the future holds for me after the study, but I don't think I could bring myself to leave Carter or take him from Zach for long periods of time. That means that I will probably be making Missouri my home again. It also means that I will probably adjust my work goals, not doing as much active research and just more programming and design. Hell, depending on the results of this study I may be able to sell my product to a large farming company and retire at thirty-two. I know, I know, keep dreaming Danni.

After lunch mom and dad ask to go to the bakery for

dessert, but I know they just want to check in on their legacy. When they finally realized that Garret and I weren't interested in baking, they took advantage of Angela being my best friend and loving the time we spent in the shop. I always knew that they'd pass the shop onto her, but she refused to take it without purchasing it from them. Weeks drug on where they argued and negotiated terms. I had never seen such a negotiation where the seller wanted a lower amount than the buyer, but Angela was family and they felt guilty charging her at all. What Angela doesn't know is that they took every dime she paid them and put it in a savings account with her name on it. They listed her in their will and testament to receive the account along with a few other items.

When we enter the The Rolling Pin Angela is waiting on a line that nearly extends out the door. When mom notices that she is working alone she taps dad's shoulder and nods to behind the counter. They both step in like they never left, they put aprons on and dad grabs the coffee pot to make his way through the small seating area. Mom takes over at the register as Angela packages desserts from the showcase. Pride fills my heart and I feel a little more at home.

After about 45 minutes, the bakery settles down. Mom and Dad are able to catch up with Angela and she of course has them taste the kringles. She leaves out the story of why she is making them, instead tells them that she just wanted to try something new.

"These are divine. They remind me of that little bakery we visited in Racine. Remember that dear, when we went to visit your sorority sisters."

"Yes! You know Angela, Wisconsin is known for their kringles and yours are just as good. I dare to say better." Mom would never lie about the quality of pastries, even to Angela.

Angela's cheeks flush, but I know it isn't from the compliments my parents are giving her. It is all about making a dessert for the man that just walked into the bakery.

"I'll be right back, duty calls." Angela rushes behind the counter and welcomes Oliver to the bakery. Everyone around the table continues their conversations, but I am focused on my best friend.

"Did I just hear that you finally made a kringle?"

"I did, but they aren't for sale yet."

"Why is that?" Oliver's relaxed tone is flirty, and causes Angela to stumble over her thoughts.

"Well, I… I uh.. I don't know if they are good enough."

"I can help you determine that. I am a self-proclaimed kringle expert. Eaten them my whole life."

"Umm.. you don't have to do that. I can have other people help me."

"Why Miss Angela, are you afraid I won't like your kringle?" His smirk implies that he isn't just talking about the pastry anymore. I step in to save my friend, from herself that is.

"That is exactly what she is afraid of. They are delicious. After eating at least two a day everyday since your first visit, I can proudly say there isn't a better one in town."

"Her opinion doesn't count. She has to say that she's my best friend."

"Get a grip, Ang. Give the man a kringle. I highly doubt your ability to make his favorite dessert will be the reason he does or doesn't ask you out…. eventually."

"DANNI!" Angela's face is a bright red, but Oliver and I chuckle while she bags a kringle and hands it to him. "It's on the house. Have a great afternoon." She rushes him away from the counter.

Oliver thanks her and winks at me before he exits the

bakery. Once he is gone Angela throws a towel at me, but I catch it with the hand I am not holding Carter with.

The bell above the door rings again, but this time it isn't Angela who catches her breath, it is Garret. Avery strides through the door to pick up her desserts for tonight's guest at the B&B, Garret never takes his eyes off of her. While Angela is in the back getting her order Avery comes to our table to say hello.

"Hello Mr. and Mrs. Graham. It is so nice to see you. What brings you to town this time of year?"

"Celebrations. We had to meet our new grandson. Also, we have to clean a few things out of the house now that Garret will be staying there full time."

"Oh?" Avery's eyes snap to where Garret is sitting, yearning for an explanation.

"We are a little sad we won't see him as often, but we support him during the change."

"What change is that?" Her voice is under control but the tapping of her index finger on the outside of her thigh shows her nerves.

"I bought a plane. I am going to give flying lessons." Garret holds her gaze, hoping to see some sort of happiness with his choice.

"Good for you. Any particular reason?" She's probing and Zach and I are the only ones that have a clue of what's going on. I instinctively place my hand on his leg under the table, nervous about how my brother will respond, knowing that the next words that come out of his mouth will set the tone for this relationship they both want but are afraid to admit to. Zach grabs my hand as if he understands and shares the same concerns.

"Family. I have a nephew now. I need to be here for him."

What a dumbass.

YOU!

He should have said YOU!

Zach squeezes my hand and draws my attention to him. He shakes his head, warning me not to butt in.

"I see." The light in Avery's eyes fades a little, but her heartbreak is interrupted when Angela brings her boxes. "I guess I'll be seeing you around then. If you have business cards I can put some at the B&B for you. Nice seeing you Mr. and Mrs. Graham." Then she is gone.

HAVING everyone at the house is exhausting. It has been years since we have all been together and my mom is insisting on a large dinner with all the fixings and guests to eat it. She says it is an early Thanksgiving since we won't all be together then, but the truth is Mom doesn't need an excuse to bring the people she loves together. Mom and Celia have gone to the store to get all the ingredients while Dad, Garret, and Zach are talking about the plane. Carter is asleep in the bassinet in the living room with the guys, so I decide to take a ride.

It doesn't take long for me to saddle Kash up to ride, I am not as out of practice as when I first got here. At first I just let go and wander where the earth takes me, but before I know it I am once again at the Turner Family Cemetery. After tying Kash to a branch I pay my respects to Mr. and Mrs. Turner, but the real reason I am here is Elizabeth.

Standing in front of her headstone tears begin to form in my eyes. My heart hurts for the pain she endured before Zach saved her. The emptiness I am sure she felt sleeping in a home with a man who didn't love her, no matter how safe she was. The life she lost giving birth to my son. A sacrifice she didn't know she was making.

"I owe you an apology. When I first saw this stone, rage took over. I was jealous because I thought you were able to make the man I loved and wanted fall for you. I was angry he threw away everything we had, our future, but gave it to you. Then I hated you because you stole my experience of carrying my son. It didn't matter that you didn't do it on purpose or that you didn't even know about it. You carried my son, felt the kicks, designed the nursery, named my baby boy. I absolutely hated you.

I am sorry.

Thank you.

Thank you for carrying my son, for sacrificing your life to give him one.

Thank you for designing a nursery because you loved him.

Thank you!"

The ride back to the barn is quick as I let Kash run freely. The cool wind dries the tears on my cheeks and my hair whips at my face. I will need to clean up before I go back to the main house, so I go to the cabin instead. Before I go upstairs to shower, I pull the bottle of whiskey out of the back of the freezer. Accepting this life is a good enough reason for a drink today. I down the glass and make my way upstairs.

Twenty-One

ZACH

Mrs. Graham has prepared a spread that could feed a high school football team. I wouldn't be surprised if she made every dish that she has in her little cookbook. She is a wonderful cook and she rarely gets the opportunity to make big meals like this anymore. Luckily for her we have a lot of people we love in this little town to invite over and they are starting to arrive. I find her in the kitchen pulling the last pie out of the oven with a huge smile on her face.

"You know, you could have had Angela bring a pie from the bakery. Saved you a bit of time." I kiss her cheek and then she swats me with her towel.

"And you know that making your favorite peach pie is not something I would leave to anyone else. Even if that someone was taught by me." Mrs. Graham flashes the same smile she passed onto her daughter. It is one of many resemblances they have passed down from her indigenous heritage.

"Peach? Let's just put that over here, no need to take it

out where everyone can eat it." When I reach for the pie she walks around the large kitchen island to avoid me as she scolds me about sharing.

Even with a full house the head of the table and the seat opposite remain empty, reminding me of all the great things my family has done to get this farm to where it is now, and I am about to give away a piece of it. I am in awe seeing the ones I love around the table for the first time in ages, this house truly feels like a home. I am brought back to reality when I hear the clink of silver on glass.

"Excuse me, everyone. I'd like to make a toast." Mr. Graham stands tall, winks at his wife and continues talking. "This town is a beautiful place, it is where we raised our children, where we built our bakery, and where we felt a part of something bigger than just ourselves. Each one of you holds a special place in our hearts and we thank you for letting us use your home Zach to host a get together for the ones we love. Retirement has suited us well, but now we get to be grandparents and we can't think of anywhere else we would rather be than here."

Claps ensue around the room, but I am focused on Danni. This is news to her, and the way she is staring at her mom proves she doesn't know what the hell just happened. After a few moments of shock, Danni finally speaks. "You are coming back?"

"We are." Her mom grabs her hand, "Is that okay with you?" Danni throws her hands around her mother's neck and tears begin to fall down her beautiful face. Another ember of hope lights inside me, just maybe she will stay after the study also.

The reunion has brought joy into my home, a feeling that has been missing for a while now. Danni is thrilled that her parents will be here to see her raise our son, even if it is currently only planned for the next two years. Each piece of this puzzle is continuing to provide me with a little more hope.

"I guess this is as good a time as any, I have some news too." I stand looking at those around the table, silence falling around me, all of them wondering what I could be saying in front of everyone without calculated thoughts. There has only been one other time that I have made a public declaration and the ring that was a part of it sits in the safe in the cabin.

"Danni and I have made arrangements to stay in the cabin with Carter, which means that Aunt Celia will be in the big house all by herself. I don't think I can handle raising two boys right now, so Mr. and Mrs. Graham, I would love for you to move in here. Garret can keep your house as he had planned and you will be here with your grandson." Garret punches my arm when he realizes the dig I made towards him, but everyone else laughs.

"Also, Andy, do you have a dollar?" Confusion crosses his face but he digs out his wallet and passes me one. I shove it in my pocket, "Great, you're fired. Lilly, you can still work for me, but only until you give Danni all the passwords."

"Zach, that isn't necessary, I told you we would let you know how things went in Idaho. We don't even have a farm yet." Andy is frustrated and I let him stew for a minute before I start to feel bad. Being in this situation with a baby on the way is enough to break a man.

"Oh that.... you do. You just purchased CJ Farms, well 99% of it. The other 1% will be yours after Danni completes the study, along with any benefits and technology of the study." His eyes move from me to Danni, who is shaking her head yes. Lilly stands and moves towards me and I think she is going to slap the shit out of me, but instead her arms squeeze my neck and she kisses my cheek. Andy follows up with a handshake, and promises to give more money than the dollar. I interrupt his vow with a hearty, "Let's eat!"

The remainder of dinner is spent catching up and telling stories about the adventures everyone has had while away. Laughter fills the house and the beer and wine bottles accumulate in the trash can. After hours of entertainment people start heading towards the empty bedrooms in the house. It isn't safe for anyone but Lilly to drive so the rooms fill quickly and Danni takes Carter to the cabin.

Garret and I clean up the remaining bottles and take the trash out. The night is cold, but the crisp air is refreshing. Both of us stand and take in the silence for a moment, wondering who is going to break first.

"So, mom and dad are moving back?" What a cop out, Garret and Danni are similar in that way. They break awkward silences with any topic that can help them avoid the conversation they don't want to have, but he didn't think this one through.

"Yeah, and living on my farm so you can keep the house. Imagine trying to sneak Avery up the lattice at 32. You're welcome man." I take another drink of my beer, but ensure he sees my smile.

"Fuck off man." He laughs, "remember the time sophomore year when I tried to sneak Jenny in. She tried to climb them in flip flops and fell down into moms rose bushes."

"I don't know who got hurt worse, Jenny from the thorns, or you from your mom. Those bushes were her pride and joy, even over you."

"Nah, Danni has always been their favorite. She didn't do stupid shit like I did." He is right that Danni was the golden child, but Mrs. Graham has always had a soft spot for her baby boy.

"She is perfect isn't she." I take the last drink of my beer and toss it in the can. "I'm going to go help her with Carter. I saw Avery head to the loft, maybe you should sneak up there. Use the stairs though bro."

When I get back to the cabin Danni is sitting in front of the open safe with the wooden box to her side. There are envelopes and papers covered in my hand writing spread across the floor. The one she is holding now is written on hotel stationary, and I know which one it is without having to look over her shoulder.

Danni,

I landed in D.C. this morning. It has been six months since you left. Really it has been six months since I fucked up and pushed you away. I thought that I could come here and change your mind. Confess how stupid I was and get you to forgive me. I had this huge plan to try and win you back. I told my dad that I was going to move out here if I was lucky enough to get you to forgive me. He said I don't have a chance. That some intelligent guy has already swept you off your feet and I will be heading back to the farm with my tail between my legs. I should have known that he'd be right.

I got your address from Garret, don't be mad at him. He was just trying to fix what he thought was his fault. You probably don't know what that means, but if I ever get the chance I will let you know. I buzzed your apartment and no one answered so I went to the coffee shop across the street and sat there for hours waiting for you to come home. Finally, you did. Except you weren't alone when you got out of the cab. You held your heels in one hand and wrapped your other in his. My dad was right.

So I have changed my flight back to Missouri to tonight. I just want to say that I am sorry for all the pain I caused, and I hope he gives you everything that I didn't.

As Always

Danni clutches the letter to her chest and lets out a sob. I told her about the letters to try and get some brownie points, it was a selfish act. Now that she is reading them she is just living through the hurt over and over again. Most of the letters were written in the first year after she left, but some of them are as recent as three months ago.

I wrote to her knowing she'd never read them, but still needing to talk to her. The day my dad died, the day I got married to Elizabeth, the day we found out Carter was a reality, all the days that I needed her but didn't deserve her, so I wrote. The last envelope in the pile is a legal sized one, it isn't as much a letter but full of documents for her to take care of Carter.

I never closed our old bank account that we had together,

never took another dime from it. I wanted her to always have it if it was needed. So I went to the bank and added Carter's name the moment I found out he was hers. I put an additional $250,000 in it and took my name off of it. I had emailed her the account number, hoping she would recognize it, but she never responded.

Along with the banking information are some papers I had my lawyer draw up to change Carter's birth certificate to showcase his true mom on the papers and a copy of the deed to show that her name was still on the cabin and the rental home so she could decide what she wanted to do with them.

She hasn't opened the envelope yet, and I don't know if she can handle it tonight so I clear my throat to let her know I am in the room. She looks at me, eyes puffy and red from crying and still the most beautiful woman I have ever laid eyes on. I reach out a hand to help her up off the floor, once she is standing she wraps her arms around my waist and continues to cry. I brush the hair, wet from her tears, away from her face but hold her until she stops and looks up at me.

The longing in her eyes tells me all I need to know. I also know that we can't start a just sex relationship without breaking our hearts, and she has told me over and over again that she will never trust me with hers. She stretches up to stand on her toes, pulling me down with her hands that are now wrapped around my neck. She whispers in my ear, "I think I need to stop drinking."

"Oh yeah, why is that?" I don't even need her to answer before my cock starts to throb against my jeans.

"Alcohol makes me do things I know I shouldn't. Like right now, I am going to ask you something, actually I am going to beg for something, just the way you like it."

"Fuck, Danni, what are you doing? We set ground rules."

"Well, I'd like to revisit those rules. We are Carter's

parents, we live in the same house and we are married to our jobs. We both have needs, let's use each other to find release." This is a horrible idea. One of us is bound to get hurt, and I know it will be me, but I can't stand the thought of another man's name on her lips."

"Name your stipulations Sweetheart."

She steps back, points to the letters. "No more bringing up the past. It is too messy. My focus is on Carter and the study, so no time for a relationship. Just sex."

I know damn well it will never be just sex, I felt the connection when I had her tied up with my belt. "Just sex? Seems like a dangerous road for us. How do you keep it just sex?"

"No pet names, you do not get to call me baby or sweetheart."

"I'm out. Those are not names I called you outside of sex. We have our ways of fucking and if we can't do it that way, I don't want in on it. If it is going to be vanilla bullshit, I'll fuck my hand."

"Who said anything about vanilla?"

"Listen, Dannielle, no nicknames right. If you want just sex, that is fine. We won't do anything outside of that, but the sex will be what it has always been. Kinky, hot, and mind blowing. You either get all of me with it or none."

She walks off and I sigh with relief. Just sex is a bad idea, and we both know it. I am glad she didn't cave for my heart, but my cock is pissed. A few deep breaths and I have calmed down enough to know that I won't march into her room and cave to her demands, so I am comfortable enough to turn around and start walking to mine.

"Fucking Christ Danni!" She is standing at the top of the stairs in a white lace bra and thong. A pair of fuck me red high heels top off the outfit, and everything I just did to calm down goes out the window.

"Come on baby, I want to play." Using the word tells me that she is giving in, she is taking the all part of the all or nothing ultimatum. Can I handle it though? How long will it be before I realize that just sex isn't enough?

Fuck it.

Twenty-Two

DANNI

I didn't want to leave Carter, but I had already been in Missouri longer than I initially anticipated. My plane took off from Kansas City 20 minutes ago, and I was lucky enough to find a nonstop flight to Ronald Reagan Airport. I follow my typical routine that keeps me from getting sick, flagging down the attendant for bottled water and opening my computer to get to work. The number of notifications on my emails instantly drives me mad. Since I have found out about being a mom I have taken parental leave and have been forbidden from working by our human resources department. It hasn't stopped everyone else from working and including me on emails though.

Initially the company wanted me to take twelve weeks and delay the start of the study. However, with the parameters I need the study to start in January and didn't want to delay an entire year. I assured them that my situation with my son would be arranged by the end of the year and I would start the study on the current schedule. I did not tell them that my son lived on the farm that the study was encompassing. I was afraid they would think I picked the farm due to personal bias.

I do read and reply to a few emails regarding my housing arrangements for the next two years. The study budget includes a flat rate for my housing expenses in my salary, but thanks to the cabin I won't need it. I will put the money in a savings account for Carter to use for college or whatever he decides when he is older.

I also read the email with the article they plan to publish about the chosen farm. I always hate reading about myself, people always write about me like I am more important than I actually am. The awards and accolades don't mean anything to me. I do what I do because I love farming and coding. My favorite award is being asked to speak to young girls around the world, encouraging them to follow whatever dreams they have even if it is in a male dominated field.

Before I know it my plane lands, and thanks to my light packing I get a quick exit from the airport. I find my Uber and head straight to my loft in Georgetown. It was the perfect place for me to live. It came fully furnished and the area is beautiful and feels like a small town. Over the years I have collected some decorations and knick knacks from local fairs and such, but I still have so little personal items all my boxes fit in my Jeep.

With the short flight and minimal packing I decide to head out on my 17 hour journey back to Missouri tonight. Typically I like to take off for long drives in the morning, but I want to get back to my son. I will have to stop for a hotel at some point, so I might as well get as much driving done as I can today. I tried to convince Angela to come with me so we could split the drive, but she has a wedding she needs to prepare for this weekend and couldn't take the time off. Zach also offered, but after the last three days of crazy sex I figured this would be a good time to step back and reflect on my poor choices.

I have made sure to send the appropriate texts to everyone when my flight took off and landed. I know that my mom and Angela will both call as soon as I tell them I have started driving, but I want to take this time to just reflect and focus on my life. I still need to let someone know I am traveling so I shoot Garret a text.

Me: I am going to drive a few hours tonight. Will text you when I stop for the night.

Me: I need some time, so don't tell anyone.

Garret: Got it! Text me every hour until you stop.

Me: Every hour? Seems excessive.

Garret: Well it is going to be dark, and I know how you get.

Me: You act like we are twins or something.

Love you. See you soon.

For the last 45 minutes I have been listening to my favorite podcast about women in tech, but my mind isn't there. I keep thinking back to Zach and picturing the way his head looks between my legs, or the way he wraps my dark hair around his wrist when he is thrusting from behind. Clearly I need something else to occupy my time.

I tune my speakers to play an audio book by a self-published author that Avery recommended. I have never heard of her before but Avery swears it is the best one she has read in ages. Apparently she blew up on social media and now they are making a movie adaptation. Avery challenged me to pretend I am scoring the movie and make a soundtrack. She wants to see how accurate I am when the movie actually comes out.

The book is hot, and so is the sound of the voice of the man who is reading it. I wanted to get my mind off Zach and the sex, but all this book has done is make me replace Zach in those images with the male lead of the book. Luckily for me the description of the character differs enough that I create my own image, with only minute similarities to Zach. I have also made a mental note of songs that fit the storyline and will be sure to add them to a playlist for Avery.

I text Garret to let him know that I made it to Pittsburgh and will be staying for the night. It leaves me about 13 hours of driving tomorrow, so although it is only about six I grab a bite to eat and try to relax. I want to get up early and continue my drive. The faster I get home, the more time I have with Carter.

I have never liked hotel showers, especially budget

friendly ones. The water is never hot enough and the pressure never strong enough. I have also always had a thing about showering in places that don't belong to me. Even with all my traveling I have never overcame they way it gives me the heebie jeebies and I still wear flip flops. A hot shower always relaxes me and helps me fall asleep, the lukewarm trickle that I just stood under did not. Therefore, I lay in the hotel bed scrolling through social media to try and fall asleep. Before I know it I am looking at pictures from our trip to New Mexico, the largest hot air balloon festival in the United States. And damn did we make it hot.

I close my eyes and recall the way that Zach instructed the Aeronaut to turn around. *Zach pulled me towards him, my back pressed against his chest. One hand slid into the opening of my dress to caress my breast, while the other creeped up my thigh and beneath my boy short underwear.*

My own hand creeps up my oversized t-shirt, lightly brushing my thigh and stomach on the way to massage my breasts.

I was able to stay quiet for a while, not wanting to make the Aeronaut uncomfortable. I am sure he knew what was happening, but he didn't need to hear it, that was until Zach pinched my clit and told me to stop holding back.

As the memory progresses, so does my self pleasure. All of my toys are packed away, so my hand will have to work tonight. I try to imitate what Zach does to me, knowing it won't be enough or even close to the same.

There was no way that he was going to let me come quietly. I arched my back resting my head on his shoulder and used my right arm to bring his lips down to mine. He matched the rhythm of his tongue to his fingers plunging into me, coating them with my desire as I came for the man two thousand feet in the air.

I begin to loose control as the memory does more for me than my hand, I was already wet and ready before I ever touched myself. I come on my fingers as I remember doing the same to Zach. I don't open my eyes until I suck my fingers clean the same way I did to him. Maybe now I will sleep well.

I SLEPT like shit last night. I woke up multiple times throughout the night stressing about not being with Carter. The last time I woke up it was only three in the morning, but I said fuck it and started driving again. The cool morning wind passes through my windows, rustling the plastic leaves of the plants that sit in my passenger seat. I stopped at a gas station and purchased enough snacks to get me through until I had to stop for a restroom break, probably longer with the amount of coffee I was going to have to drink to stay alert.

Again I text Garret to let him know I was on the road, I don't expect him to text back with it being so early, but my notification goes off within seconds.

Zach: Drive safely. We need you.

I DOUBLE CHECK to make sure I actually texted Garret and not Zach. I certainly don't need to send him a message telling him I love him. A sense of relief hits me when I see my text was delivered to the correct person. I am sure Zach is just up feeding Carter and took the opportunity, he probably thinks I am still asleep and will see the message when I wake. It doesn't stop me from over analyzing the text.

We said it was just sex, just a release. Saying things like "we need you" is taking things deeper. I can't allow my heart to be broken again, so last time has to be the last time. A sigh escapes me, my heart breaks a little with the realization and I accept that the next two years have to be professional only.

After a few hours of driving and listening to podcasts I stop again, this time I text everyone to let them know I am driving. Let the games begin to see who can call first. It doesn't take long before Angela's name is popping up on my screen.

"Good morning Bestie."

"Why are you so happy? It is six in the morning and you're driving all alone." She clearly hasn't had her first cup of coffee.

"I have been driving for hours, but I didn't want to wake anyone. I text Garret to let him know."

"I see how it is, I have one wedding so I have to stay home and you replace me with your brother."

"I'm sure you had a long night. I didn't want to wake you." I chuckle. "Anyway, did you check on Carter like I asked?"

"You do know that Zach and Celia are there right. That they have been taking care of that baby since day one?"

"Angela," I hate knowing that I haven't been in my son's life the entire time. It makes me feel like Zach has leverage on me or something, even though I know that he would never think of it that way. I have lost time to make up for and I am already gone again. "You know what I mean."

"Yes, I have checked on him. I held him, read to him, fed him, and watched him sleep. All the things a cool aunt does. Now let's get to the real topic at hand."

I haven't told her that Zach and I have been sleeping together. She would scold me for sure. It isn't that she doesn't want us together, she will be glad to tell you that we should be, especially now that we have Carter. However, she would be pissed at me for trying to say it is only sex when I know damn well it never could be.

"You're right, how did Oliver like the kringle?"

"You know that isn't the topic I was talking about Danni!" I can hear her smile in her voice, and know that she wants to say something, but that fucking douche messed with her head enough I don't know that she will ever trust someone in the love department ever again.

"I know, but did he like it?"

"I'd be willing to bet the bakery he didn't. He has been back twice but he buys a kringle and something else every time. He clearly didn't like it and is only buying it to spare my feelings."

"Or he did like it and buys it because they are absolutely divine." Everything that Angela bakes is delicious, so much so that I even try things that include ingredients I don't like. "I think he likes the kringle and is trying other items you make because he likes you."

I hear her exasperated sigh, "Or maybe he is buying something for someone else, a girlfriend or wife."

"Not everyone is your dicktree ex husband Angela!" She grumbles and I know that she doesn't want to believe all men are the same, and she likes Oliver enough not to argue about it so I give in. "I slept with Zach." I try to keep my tone calm and even to give her no indication of how it is affecting me.

"Excuse me?"

"More than once." I bite down in embarrassment even though I know she can't see me.

"Danni! I mean he is the father of your child, but when

did you get back together and why am I just now hearing about it."

"We didn't get back together. It is just sex —"

She cuts me off at the comment. "Good lord Dannielle, how stupid can you actually be. I take that back, what the fuck is going through your head? Were you drunk? High? This isn't a good idea and you know it."

"I know, that is why when I get back I am going to tell him that I can't do it anymore. I was horny, what can I say? It had been three years since I touched a man, or worse since a man had touched me Ang. I needed something and I didn't want to have to deal with a stranger and the drama."

"The drama of a stranger? Do you hear yourself? No drama could be worse than the shit you just opened up. I can't believe you would lie to yourself or him and say it is just sex." She is right, I knew it wasn't just sex before it happened, for either of us, but I couldn't help it. Maybe I secretly wanted it to be more. Maybe I lied to myself because I thought I could make him fall in love with me again and we could be the perfect family.

"I know," is all I can say.

"Danni, when you guys split, I was there for you. I watched you break and throw yourself into your job. I helped play your game of temptation when you came home, but I need you to know something. Zach broke too. The only difference was that the whole town was angry at him while he did it. He didn't get the same support, he dealt with it on his own. Even Celia was pissed."

There is a brief moment of silence while I mull over what she is saying. I never thought about how it impacted him, how could I when he hurt me so bad? Now I know the truth and it is killing me inside that he hurt that way, that everyone blamed him for my pain and he had to sort is shit out alone.

"He called me after he saw you in Washington. He gave up then, saying he ruined it for good. That you were happy with another man and he couldn't blame you. He asked me to let him know when you got married, but not until after. He didn't trust himself to not go and confess his love one last time. I was still angry with him, so I didn't tell him that I knew you weren't with anyone, at least seriously."

"I uhh…… I gotta go my mom is calling, You know how she gets when I am driving and don't answer. Talk soon." My mom isn't calling, and I am pretty sure Angela knows that, but I can't listen to this anymore. I need something else to occupy my mind, and I don't want to admit that she is right.

"Danni, before you decide to do this or not, know that it won't ever be just sex for either of you. That doesn't mean you both don't deserve what it can be, but talk about it with Zach." The silence of the line lets me know she has hung up. I keep it that way, no podcast, no audio book, no highway country.

Twenty-Three

ZACH

I run my hands through my wet hair and let the water pour down my face. The moment that I close my eyes I am reliving my last shower experience with Danni. My hands lay flat against the tile at the end of extended arms as I hold my head under the water trying to compose myself. I drift deeper into the memory.

I AM STANDING in my boxer briefs brushing my teeth when I hear the door open. It has been a fucking day, I lost two calves to an idiot who cut my fence, and I had to show him what it means to fuck with Turner Farms. When you play stupid games, you get stupid fucking prizes. This prize included a few broken bones and could have been worse if Danni didn't call to check in.

The sweet aroma of her hits me before her arms wrap around my waist just above the towel. Her soft lips pepper kisses along my shoulder blades as her finger tips dance across my skin. Every ounce of me wants to read in to the intimate connection, but I know I can't. Danni will never love me the way that she used to, and I agreed to her stupid fucking game of just sex.

As I bend my waist to rinse my mouth she steps away and turns on the shower. While the water heats her eyes lock with mine in the mirror, first she removes her shirt, then her jeans, leaving her standing in nothing but cotton panties and a bra. It shouldn't be sexy, but damn she doesn't even have to try.

My knuckles grip the sink, I refuse to be the first to react. This game is something I have come accustomed to over the last few days. The more I resist, the more anger fuels her drive. Less feelings, more kinks.

"I am just going to get cleaned up before bed." She smirks and unclasps her bra.

"In my shower. The one in room isn't good enough for you now?" Still facing the mirror I am able to view her reaction, while hiding mine that continues to grow under the towel.

"Eh, the water isn't as hot." Her left shoulder meets her ear as her upper lip curls while she tries to play off the innuendo.

"Do I need to leave you a t-shirt on the bed too, maybe the cotton is softer on this side of the house?" My fingers begin to tingle from the strength of my grip.

"I sleep better naked, but maybe I'll try your sheets." With that she steps into the shower. I take a deep breath before I turn to walk away, but she interrupts my escape. "I forgot my body wash in my room. Do you mind? Her words are nonchalant to the naked ear, but to me it's an invite.

I return with the body wash within minutes. The doors to the oversized shower are covered with steam, but I can still see the outline of her curves. The blurred vision reminds me of our current relationship, and I know deep down I am running out of time. I don't know what will happen first, she remembers that she hates me or I tell her I need more, either way this ends.

I open the shower fully intending to drop the soap on the shelf and leave, but my dick disagrees. Danni is facing the wall as the water runs down her body, her long dark hair slicked back and plastered like an arrow point straight down to her plump ass. I have to play this right, my heart wants me to walk in and shower her with soft touches and cover her body with my lips, but my heart will lead to destruction.

Instead I drop my towel and enter quickly, I place one hand around her waist bracing her as I push her upper body towards the wall. She catches herself with her hands, I wrap her hair in my left hand pulling her head back so my mouth is next to her ear. A soft moan escapes her, and I smirk.

"Tell me, do you like to break my rules?" I growl as my right hand smacks her ass causing her to whimper. She spreads her feet in a sign that she wants more.

"You will not be a fucking dick tease Danni." My hand tightens on her hair, my teeth scrape her ear, her ass raises in anticipation, but I don't smack it. "You don't like it do you. Me coming in here, getting you ready to fuck and backing off." My statement lets her know that I can fuck with her just as much as she does me. "Now I have to get dried off again." My tone imitates irritation and I release her then head to the door of the shower, I won this round and she is about to make her move to prove it.

She presses her body against my back again within seconds, her hand reaches around grabbing my cock. She gives me a few pumps before she walks around to my front. She pushes on my chest to knock me back under the water, "not until I make you come."

I swipe my hand over my face again at the memory, but

my other hand is already stroking my length. It is the fourth time I have fucked my hand since she left, less than twenty-four hours ago. Not once did I look at her pictures or videos from the gift. I just closed my eyes and I replay what has happened since I saw her on the stairs in the white lace bra and panties with killer red heels.

Knowing this is a losing battle I stroke my length until my lower back tingles and my come splatters the tiles on the shower wall. I reach for the soap and once again clean my body. "Fuck! Get your shit together man."

THE WEATHER IS GETTING COOLER and the days shorter as time passes. It is a little after three in the morning and I just texted Danni to let her know to drive safe and how much we need her here. I don't expect a response, as I am sure she is still asleep, but I need her to know that she is the first thing I think of when I wake up, I just can't say it yet.

My phone vibrates on the counter next to my coffee cup, and my heart leaps for a moment. Is she thinking about me too? I flip over the phone to see Andy's name on the screen, shit what the fuck is going on now.

"What now, Andy?" There is never a good reason he would call at this time.

"Fucking Idiots, sir. A couple guys found another prick trying to steal cattle."

"Which field?" I know it shouldn't matter, but it does. A location tells me more information than the thief would like. I will be able to figure out how he accessed my land and maybe try to determine the motive.

"It's the Angus boss." Andy continues, "We got the prick. He is in the tack room. Would you like me to wait on you?"

"No, you keep working and make sure the guys keep their mouth shut. I don't need the sheriff knowing if I am going to handle this myself."

"Got it boss." Andy hangs up as I toss my phone onto the counter. I am not quite sure what I did to get this kind of karma the last few weeks, but I sure as hell pissed off someone.

The old me would have rushed straight to the tack room and used my favorite form of manipulation to get answers. The new me is a dad, and a dad that would like the mother of his child to stick around. I hold off on business, instead I go to my son's room. I watch him sleep in his crib, his little thumb in his mouth, the picture of peace. I am a different man because of him, more aware of dangerous situations, dare I say a little fearful of what dangers I could bring to the ones I love. Because of that I make my way to the tack room with negotiation on my mind instead of violence.

Twenty-Four

ZACH

My typical tactics didn't sit on the back burner very long. I sat for twenty minutes trying to get the man to speak. When he continued to stare at me I had to revert back to what I know best.

"Tell me who you're working for!" I give the prick ten seconds to answer before my fist finds his jaw. "Is it really worth your life?"

The man spits blood, "If you don't kill me he will."

"What does he want with my cattle?" His silence is broken by the sound of my knuckles crashing into his ribs. "This can be quick and easy, or long and agonizing. Your choice."

The man's body slouches as he continues to lose strength, his hands chained above his head in an old barn far enough away from the house that people can't hear his screams. This isn't the first time I have had to deal with assholes trying to sabotage my farm, but it has never gone this far. An hour ago a few of my hands found this fool trying to steal a few of my heifers. Not just any heifers either, my best Angus set to sell later this month. The circumstances make me think it is more than just a jilted employee or tenant. "Who did I piss off this time? An old employee that I paid well above anyone else around here? A tenant that I gave multiple chances before I had to evict them?"

The man chuckles, "Why don't you ask your little slut? Maybe she can point you in the right direction." I'm baffled, I have no idea what his man is talking about, but I can't let him see it. No one knows about me and Danni so he certainly can't be talking about her. Elizabeth is dead, but maybe her ex doesn't know that. Is this fucker really trying to come back years after I ran his ass out of town?

"So you work for that coward who wasn't man enough to take care of something good, and I had to take it from him?"

"You could say that." The man spits blood again, this time trying to aim it in my direction, but his body is weak. He will pass out at any minute and I need information. "Or your greedy bitch couldn't be satisfied with what he could give her."

"Dean is a piece of shit. I told him when I helped Elizabeth get away from his abusive ass, that if he ever stepped foot in this county again he'd live to regret it. Clearly he is still a coward and sent you to do his dirty work. Which county line is he hiding behind?" The look on the man's face shows confusion, is he just realizing the piece of shit he is working for beat the person he supposedly loved?

"Who the fuck is Dean?" His head drops with the question, he's out cold. I unchain him from the hanging post and lock him in what used to be a tack room, now a holding room. I pick up the phone and call the one person that I hate dragging into shit, but know that his temper matches mine. He also happens to have a few friends that help me track things that cops won't give me access to.

"Hey man, what's up? You ready to work on that Mustang? Danni being gone must be eating at ya?" His voice is too chipper and he's being the typical smart ass, he's in a good mood and I am about to fuck it up. Why do I always bring chaos to the people I care about most?

"Not quite." I'm curt and I let him assess the mood on his own before I continue. "I need you and Cable. When can you get to the Tack Room?"

"Shit, okay man." I can hear the change in his voice and he knows this is serious. "I'll be there in five. I'll call Cable on the way."

Cable is a tech genius that Garret met during an investigation into the FAA. Cable had been caught in a string of cyber attacks by Homeland, but was turned into an asset to catch other criminals in action. Someone had hacked into the FAA system and was deleting or altering flight manifest sheets and leaving a trail that connected Garret to some major crimes. Once Garret was pulled in, questioned, and cleared, him and Garret became good friends. Now Cable is our go to when we need to go around the law.

When Garret arrives I am leaning against the tailgate of my truck. Between the phone call and arrival his demeanor has changed, he doesn't know what is going on but he is already pissed. It has always been this way, if I am mad he is ten times that for me and vice versa. We are brothers and you just don't fuck with that. While he was getting pissed about someone doing something to me, I was going over every body language cue the douche in the tack room gave off, every word he said, and I think this has nothing to do with

Elizabeth and everything to do with Danni. Which means that as mad as Garret is now, it is about to get worse.

I fill him in on what happened from the point my men found the dick on my land to now and he lets me know that Cable is being flown in by one of their chopper buddies and will arrive in about thirty minutes. While we wait we ride up to the area my men found the thief to check for clues.

"You really think this is where someone would come to steal your cattle if they didn't want to get caught? Or was getting caught part of the plan to send you a message?" Garret looks at me with anger and a bit of fear in his eyes. "If this is about Danni, this douche is a pawn in a bigger game. Your cattle have nothing to do with it."

"I have thought about that, but Danni is here for the farm study. Why would someone be pissed about that and if they are, why call her a slut?"

"I don't know man. She didn't really date after you. A couple guys here and there, but her longest relationship was like three or four months. Did you check for a wallet or anything?"

"Yeah, he was clean, nothing on him that could be traceable."

"He still have his fingers?"

"I'm not fucking evil dude. I don't just go carving people up."

"Yeah, well no one has ever been a threat to the woman you love before."

My heart drops and vile rises into my throat. I had put it together that this could be about Danni, but I didn't go as far to believe it was a threat. Truth is that even threatening her study pisses me off.

"Does she have any rivals in the tech world that would try to sabotage the study?"

"She is Woman of the Year and has been recently nominated for some other nerdy ass award in the global tech world. I'm sure she has jealous assholes out there somewhere that want to see her fail."

"Any that have the funds to pay some crook to do their bidding?" I am not really expecting an answer, I know that if someone wants to take her down, they would find a way. I'm conflicted now as to if this is a jealous tech competitor or some piece of shit that is pissed he didn't get his shot with her. I'm leaning more towards a piece of shit.

We hear the chopper before we see it, and I am ready for the answers that come along with it. The downwash is loud and has me blocking my face from the dry grass being blown in my direction. Cable jumps out with a bag full of equipment and waves off the pilot, the chopper is up and gone in minutes.

"Fellas" Cable nods and waves his hand across the horizon, "A beautiful day to crack a code." He is arrogant, but he has earned it. He isn't your typical image of a tech genius, or even a criminal. If I had to guess his occupation based on looks, he'd be some kind of blue collar laborer. He is built like a farm hand, with the callouses to boot, and could be attributed to the underground fighting he does. The man is definitely someone you don't want to be on the wrong side of.

The thief is still out when I open the tack room door. We take the opportunity to scan his fingerprints before waking him up. Cable also takes a swab of his mouth and a lock of hair. He sets up and begins to analyze the information and search for answers outside of the room. I want to get as much information out of this guy before he realizes the shit we have on him.

Cable will be able to get us his personal information

quickly, but finding how he is connected to Danni will take longer. Getting it out of him will be quicker if we can make it happen. He is tied to a chair when he comes to. I am standing in the corner behind him, out of sight. Garret however is standing in front of him rolling up his sleeves as he waits for the man to gain full consciousness. But before Garret has a chance to speak, the douche laughs and shakes his head.

"You're friend finally got the point. Called in the brother to help figure out why his pretty little whore is the cause of this problem." Garret doesn't look at me, he doesn't want to give away that I am there, but we both get the confirmation we need that this is definitely about Danni.

"Whore is quite the word for someone as smart as you. Couldn't come up with anything better with your fancy college education?" Garret is probing trying to determine which angle we are fighting. "Must be a real blow to your ego to get beat out by a woman in your male driven profession. First she gets Woman of the Year, how dare they offer such an award." Sarcasm seeps through his tone. "Then she receives a nomination for Innovator of the year, a category usually only occupied by men, but she's breaking glass ceilings."

Garret waits for the man to say anything, but he remains quiet. "You didn't do your research very well. If you thought sabotaging her study would ruin her chances at winning. It is a two year long study, with a farm that has more money than you could ever dream of. You think a couple cattle are going to change things?"

"Have you ever heard of a diversion?" I want to wipe the smirk off the man's face, but I can't let him know that I am here. We still haven't figured out if this is about the study or not and how much danger Danni is truly in. My phone vibrates in my hand, letting me know Cable has something.

Cable: Brady Coats, from Birmingham. Not in Tech.

Me: How is he connected to Danni?

Cable: I'm looking

Me: If he isn't in tech the threat is worse.

Me: See if anyone he is connected to is in tech, and find out how he is connected to Danni.

Cable: Like I said I am looking.

When I make eye contact with Garret I give him the signal that we discussed prior. His body shifts as anger continues to pulse through him. This man is about to witness a rarity when it comes to Garret Graham and he better start praying to whatever god he believes in.

"So you're the bait, your boss really values your existence." Garret is trying to goat him, but it doesn't seem to be working. I text Garret the name, he can use it to let the prick know we are on to him. "Mr. Brady Coats. Hmph" Garret is remembering something, but I can tell by the look on his face he can't place it. Brady doesn't notice, he doesn't know Garret's tells the way I do.

"Well, Brady, you and I officially have a problem. You see you have come into my town, fucking with my family, and have the balls to insult my sister in front of me." Garret's right hook hits Brady so hard the chair he is tied to wobbles. "I just don't like it all that much." his tone stays calm and eerily soothing.

Brady continues to stare at the man in front of him, cocky and ignorant to the level of crazy Garret hides under his smooth exterior.

"Seems as though you don't like to talk much," Garret grabs a set of pliers and a knife off of a tray that Brady just now notices. "Not much use for a tongue then." He takes a few steps towards the man whose eyes are now large enough to pop out of his head.

In a panic he finally speaks, "That whore led my brother on for three months, then left his ass." It is the first vital information that he has given us. This has nothing to do with the farm study and everything to do with some jealous piece of shit Danni dated. I don't know how long ago it was, but the look on Garret's face says that he does.

"Brock. That was three years ago."

"He's kept tabs, he doesn't like to be made a fool."

"How long have you been in town?"

Brady is silent again, at least until Garret takes another step towards him while spinning the blade in his hand.

"I have been following her since she left my brother." Garret's boot lands square in Brady's chest, the force knocking over the chair and putting me in his sights.

Twenty-Five

DANNI

Zach's name pops up on my phone, but I decline the call. I can't have a conversation with him while I am driving. I know what needs to be said and I know it has to be done face to face. He calls again, and again I decline it. He doesn't stop, the third time I begin to worry something is wrong with Carter and I answer it.

"What is wrong with Carter?"

"Nothing, why would you say that?"

"Why else would you call three times in a row after I clearly declined the first two attempts" My tone is snippy, but he had me worried something was wrong with my son.

"I need to know where you are right now. I need you to share your location with me."

"What the fuck is wrong with you. We aren't a couple, as a matter of fact the just sex is over too. Fuck off Zach." I hang up, but my phone rings again, this time it is Garret. "Seriously, you can't even take my side this one time. You are going to work with him on this?"

"Dannielle, this is serious. Share your location. I know you left early, so you are closer than Zach knows, but I need to know how close." The fear in my brother's voice sends me into panic. He is always the happy go lucky guy with a huge personality. He is the life of the party at all the family events, but I know he has a dark side, and I can sense it through this call.

"I'm just about an hour south of home. Why?"

"How much gas do you have?"

"Garret, you are scaring me, what is going on?"

"Answer the question, Dannielle"

"About three quarters of a tank, why?"

"Listen to me very carefully, I want you to drive to the nearest police station. Tell them that you are being followed by a group of men, you don't know the vehicle ——-"

"I do, I thought it was a coincidence, but this blue Camry has been behind me for the last hundred miles or so." I don't know what the hell is going on, but my chest tightens and the hair on the back of my neck stands on end.

"We don't know if that is the only car, there may be a trap closer to home. I want you to reroute. Turn back East, remember the roads that Grampa used to take us on during those Sunday drives? Take those, you have enough gas. Then when you get in town, don't go to the farm. Go to Celia's Diner, Mr. and Mrs. Turner will meet you there. Duke will be watching for you."

Garret hangs up and I immediately share my location with both him and Zach. I don't know what the hell is happening, but it is serious. It is obvious to me that Garret thinks someone could be listening to our conversations. Our Grampa took us on boat rides on the Mighty Mo every Sunday. The river is on the West, not the East. If this guy is following me and listening then he will know that I turn off to the West instead of the East like my brother said and then Garret's plan will be foiled.

I am about ten minutes from my next exit when I see the chopper circling, Duke. Comfort and terror race through my mind. It is great to know that they have their eyes on me, but something terrible is happening if Duke is involved. Duke is a pilot friend of Garrets. He is a war vet and a man of few words, but loyal to the core.

I have to make a choice, do I keep going East, the quickest route home, or head West like my brother's cryptic message said? I remind myself that my brother has a plan and if I go against it, I risk messing up whatever they have going on. I take the exit to head west and follow the curves along the river. If there is a trap it would be set up in the expected travel path. The East comment was to stall, ensuring the trap can't move as quickly as we are and also thinking that I am headed somewhere else. They will have to search for a place called Celia's Diner, another stall tactic.

Aunt Celia lived in a little cabin out on the back of the farm when we were kids. She would always make the best meals and we would always call it Celia's Diner when we ate there. The house burned down when we were in high school, but the old picnic table was moved up by the family cemetery. That's where I am headed and I am thankful I drive a Jeep to go over the terrain. It will make it easier to outrun the asshole behind me if they have the balls to follow me onto the farm. I just hope opening the fence on the pasture was a part of their plan so I don't have to get out and attempt it on my own.

Once I hit the back roads my confidence increases and I plan to lose the car behind me. I have the knowledge and experience driving here to increase my speed. It doesn't take long before I pass a couple cars in short straight aways, putting a little distance between the creep and myself. Duke is still hovering above making sure that Garret and Zach know my exact location, but I am hoping he picks up on my next move. He needs to keep going when I pull into the woods. With the guys having my location on their phones, and the Camry still driving, Duke should easily realize what is happening.

Here goes nothing, keep tracking him Duke.

The initial jerk causes me to tense up a bit, but I have been off roading enough in the last few years that I know what to anticipate. The timber here looks like it is thick and goes on for a while from the road, but there are old pathways cleared for racing our ATVs just about twenty yards in. The tan color of the jeep blends in with the fall trees and I take the path until I get to a place I can veer off and get into the pasture. The guys won't be expecting me at the entrance so I will have to open the fence myself, but I should have bought myself enough time. Even if the Camry attempted to follow me, and there is no way he saw me turn off, he won't make it over the terrain. Looking out the window I see that Duke caught on and is continuing the original path, leading the Camry straight to Zach and Garret's trap, easing a bit of the concern that has been tight in my chest.

The sound of an engine approaches as I am opening the gate. My heart races and my fingers fumble from fear, my hand slips from the metal latch catching on the rough wood. "Shit!" There is a half inch splinter lodged into my palm, but I don't have time to get it out, I need to get the gate open and get through before whoever is headed this way catches up to me. The sound of the engine is getting closer, it is louder than a car, fuck I wasn't fast enough. They still trapped me, how? Why?

The latch opens as the four-wheeler tops the hill, I push

the gate to swing it open, and run toward my Jeep. I hear my name being yelled, but my heart pounding in my ears doesn't allow me to register who is yelling it. I am too scared to look back, afraid it will cost me precious time. Once I am next to my Jeep, I reach across the seat for my firearm that is in my center console. The engine cuts off, the man is yelling my name again, but I can't register anything but the need to protect myself. I turn around and put my gun into defense mode, I am ready to fire, if need be, but the man standing in front of me is no one to fear.

"It's me, it's me." I drop the gun into the driver seat behind me. There is blood on his hands and shirt, but I don't care. I fall into my brother's arms and tears start streaming down my face. "I've got you." After a few seconds of allowing me to catch my bearings he tells me to get in the passenger side. He calls Duke first, demanding he keep trailing the car that was following me, then Zach.

"I've got her. She is shaken up, but unharmed." He pauses to let Zach talk, listening intently but I just stare out the window. I have never been described as weak or unable to take care of myself, especially not on this land, but something feels different this time. "I don't think she needs to worry about it right now. Let's get her some place safe to relax and she can answer questions later."

He pauses again, I don't know what Zach is saying, but he isn't happy with the situation or what Garret is proposing.

"I fucking know that she is the mother of your child! I fucking know that you love her, but she is my goddamn sister!" Garret inhales deeply, "Listen man, this isn't your fault. This is about someone coming after her, you need to understand —"

"Excuse me?!" I thought this was clearly something to do with Garret or Zach and someone they pissed off and I was just a casualty of relation. "What do you mean that someone is coming after me?"

"We can talk about it once we get you somewhere safe."

"No! I am a grown ass woman, and we will talk about it now. Put the phone on speaker." He begrudgingly listens. "I don't care who fucking talks, but someone better start right now."

"My hands found a man trying to steal cattle this morning. When I brought him to the tack room he wouldn't speak. We brought in Cable to get some information. Turns out the douche was trying to create a diversion here on the farm to keep me away from you during their plan."

"What plan Zach?"

"The guy's name is Brady Coats, he's from —-"

"Alabama. I dated his brother for a few months. What does he want with me?"

"Apparently, his brother still wants you. Brady admitted that he's been ordered by Brock to tail you ever since you left him." My stomach clenches, I need to puke. Someone has been watching me for three years and I didn't even know it. "Any reason you can think of that he would strike now, after so long?"

"I'll find out. Take me to him now."

"Abso-fuckin-loutley not. I will not take my sister near the prick that is trying to harm her." Garret isn't going to budge, so I have to pull the one thing I know will work.

"Twin card."

"We aren't twelve years old Danni, this isn't a game." He is irritated that I would even try to pull the old promise out. The twin card was created because we wanted to hold each other to secrecy if one of us got in trouble, mainly him. Then as we got older it was because one of us needed something. The last time I brought it up was about two years after I left home. I was in desperate need of something familiar yet non-judgmental and convinced him to take a vacation from work and spend some time in Washington.

"If Brock wants me then I will be able to figure out why. You don't know what makes him tick, but I do." I will not let them push me away from this. I need to know what is going on and why this asshole thinks he deserves to stalk me for three years. I also don't want to tell Zach that Brock is the last man I slept with, I don't need the father of my child going to prison.

"We tried pushing her out when we thought shit was too hard for her before, she proved us wrong. I for one learned my lesson about making decisions about her without her." Zach isn't happy about agreeing with me, but he is right. Unless they lock me up somewhere I will still get my way, and it is better to include me in the plan than make me go rogue.

"If my sister gets hurt, it's your ass that I am kicking." Garret's shoulders slouch and a sigh of defeat comes over him. "We will be at the tack room in five."

Twenty-Six

DANNI

As we arrive at the tack room Zach is standing in the door. His right shoulder leans against the frame as he rubs his thumb against the opposite palm. The tell isn't one that is obvious to a stranger, but anyone that has been around Zach for more than half his life would know he is stressed and deep in thought. I don't think he even knows that he does it, similar to the way he taps his fingertips on his thigh when he is nervous.

The sound of the door closing makes him look up at me, there is guilt in his eyes. My thoughts on his tactics have always made the conversation a silent one. He did what he needed to do, and we acted like it never happened. It is the blood on his knuckles and clothes that make my stomach turn, but the sorrow in his eyes that melts my heart. Maybe there is something there.

I don't have time or energy to think about it at this point. I need to speak to Brady and I have to figure out my approach. Storming into the room with a head full of steam will not get me anywhere with this family. If I want to know where Brock is, I have to manipulate the situation, but I need to prepare Zach. This is not going to be easy for him.

"You aren't going to like what I go in here and do. Maybe you should stay out here." I walk right past him, leaving no room for argument, but the grip on my arm stops me from going further.

"I know I fucked up D. I made choices for you in the past instead of with you. I'm not going to tell you not to go in there, but I will tell you that I am coming along." His statement sounds as if he is trying to be in control while still asking for permission. I nod my head and walk into the room with both the father of my child and my brother following behind me.

Brady is beat to hell. The swelling on his face has already forced one of his eyes shut and the dried blood tells me he has been here for a decent amount of time. Between my brother and Zach, I am surprised he is still alive, which tells me that he didn't give up any information they seemed vital. It also means that Cable hasn't found Brock either.

"Brady," no response. "Brady," I speak softly and slightly nudge his shoulder. I bend down in front of him, in hope that he feels less intimidation. He doesn't speak but his eyes open. "Brady, why have you been following me? What did Brock tell you?"

Brady is ten years younger than Brock and has always looked up to his older brother. For the short amount of time I dated Brock, I was able to see how much he wanted to make him proud. He went to school to become a chef, following in Brock's footsteps. What he didn't know was that his brother was a prick who thought he could man handle women without the consequences. One night he came over to my apartment pissed about a review, when I went to give him a welcome kiss he shoved me against the wall and grabbed my throat. It took less than ten seconds for me to realize that he wasn't about to give me some hot sex, instead he was taking his anger out on me. That was the last night he saw me.

"The truth." Brady smirks, "That you are a whore and cheated on him with some nobody."

I let him continue to speak, knowing that his admiration for Brock will never be broken if I am too defensive.

"How could you? Dannielle, he loved you. We all loved you. After you cheated on him, he left and went to Paris. He took a job there to avoid running into you. It broke my mom's heart. You were supposed to be my friend."

"Oh Brady, I am your friend. Why didn't you come to me instead of following me? We could have talked about this."

"He said I couldn't. He said we were going to make you pay. That it was your fault that my family was torn apart and…"

"And what Brady?"

"My mom died when he was in Paris. The doctor told us it was a heart attack, said too much stress. It is your fault. If you didn't cheat on him, then he wouldn't have left."

I wrap my arms around the young man in front of me. The pain of losing a parent isn't something that I wish upon anyone, even the man you has been stalking me for three years. I have one shot to get him on my side, I just wish that Zach and Garret weren't standing here to see it.

"Brady, do you remember the night he called you? When he said I was cheating." I wait for him to say something but he refuses. "He was sitting on top of me, after he slammed me onto the kitchen floor." I stop to look at the men across the room. Zach is staring me down, but Garret leaves the room. I can only assume he is going to have Cable track down Brock.

"He came over pissed about work. He grabbed me by the throat and threw me against the wall. When I tried to fight back he swept my feet out from under me and slammed me against the floor. He told me that he owned me, and that another man would never touch me again." Tears begin to fill my eyes as I remember the night I haven't spoke of before.

"No, no he wouldn't. He loved you. You are just a whore and you do want to admit it."

"I've got pictures of the bruises, hell I have got copies of my security cameras that show him doing it. I can show you." My voice is stern now, I need Brady to see the man his brother truly is. "I will get my phone—" commotion outside interrupts, and I am out the door before I realize it.

"Duke followed him to the diner. Pete picked him up, cuffed him and dropped him off. ID says Brock Coats." Garret shoves the man on the ground where he falls in front of my feet. "Cable has the footage and photos from the night you were talking about. I can hand it over to Pete, or..." he cracks his knuckles, "the choice is your's Sis."

Playing games with a man's life isn't something that I want to do, but I also need to think about more than just me right now. If I let Garret and Zach take care of this they could get in a lot of trouble. If I hand it over to the law, will it be enough to put the man away forever? Will he get out and be a threat to my son? "Why would you lie to your brother?"

Brock maneuvers around to a sitting position and spits at me. He is a coward and he is going to pay for it.

"Let me tell you something sweetie. You are a mediocre chef, a shitty lay, a terrible brother, and a pathetic excuse of a man. You deserve every ounce of pain you are about to receive. You will never hit another woman again, and you will never cause your brother to pay for your mistakes."

Whatever happened after I walked away from Brock is

something I hope to never know. I did show Brady the photos and footage before I left the tack room. I hope it is enough for him to realize that he needs to be his own person and not manipulated by his piece of shit brother.

I SPENT the evening with Avery at the Bed and Breakfast. She had taken Carter to her place to keep him safe, and I just wanted to be around my son. It is amazing how just a few weeks ago I was planning my next girls trip full of sun, beaches, and shots, now I am thinking about farm to table baby food and his first Thanksgiving.

"Thank you for everything. Truly, I forgot how much home means family around here." I hug her after I secure the carseat and close the car door.

"Danni, you don't have to be home to have us as family, although I much prefer it." She squeezes me tight and holds me until I am the first to let go.

"You are coming for Thanksgiving right?" I am sure she will argue, it is tough on her to be in love with my brother and think that he doesn't feel the same way. "Carter isn't the only reason Garret is making life changes you know." With that I wink and get in the driver seat.

Avery rolls her eyes, but the small smile on her face is evidence that she is willing to accept there might be more to Garret's story. "I'll bring the green beans."

Twenty-Seven

ZACH

I have never wanted to end a man's life as much as I do today. Only a coward would ever put his hands on a woman, and he happened to hurt the woman that I love. That same love is the reason I didn't kill the piece of shit. You see, when you own damn near the entire county, you get a little pull with the law. Brock will be sentenced next week for the domestic abuse, stalking, and attempted kidnapping charges. When he gets out, if he makes it out, he will be a fool to ever fuck with my family again.

My talk with the judge kept me out later than I would like. I know that Danni is stressing about what is happening and I want get home to put her mind to ease. When I walk through the door she is snoring softly on the couch under my Grandmother's quilt. Her latest novel is clinched in her arms and the baby monitor sits on the coffee table next to an empty wine glass.

The embers in the fireplace tell me she fell asleep quite a

while ago. I place a couple more logs to stoke the fire and sit in the recliner across from the couch. I know what we had is over, it was just a matter of time, and 24 hours away was all it took. Her words from earlier are on repeat in my head.

"What the fuck is wrong with you. We aren't a couple, as a matter of fact the 'just sex' is over too. Fuck off Zach.

DURING HER TRIP she cleared her head and remembered that she hated me. I'd hate me too. I broke her heart and sent her away. I put her in the path of that bastard who blacked her eye and bruised her ribs. I thought that everything I did helped her, was what was best for her, and I let this happen to her. The rough callouses of my hand scratch my cheek as I wipe away a tear.

Danni is the strongest woman, hell the strongest person I know. She has carried this pain with her for three years, alone, refusing to be a victim. Even with all that she has been through, she is anything but fragile. She deserves the world, and I am going to make sure she gets it, even if I don't get her.

IT IS 9:00 am and Danni is still asleep. After I carried her to her room I took the baby monitor with me. She will be pissed that I didn't let her get up with Carter throughout the night, but she needed the rest.

Carter and I spent the morning at the grocery store shopping for Thanksgiving dinner. Mr. and Mrs. Graham will be wrapping things up in Florida to be moved back home before Christmas, which means Danni and I will be cooking. I know that Carter won't remember the meal, but I will and so will his mom. With everything that has happened lately she needs a little light in her life.

My phone pings as I walk down the produce aisle with a message from Danni wanting to know where we are. Instead of texting back I take the opportunity to remind her of the softer side of me. I dial her number and click FaceTime.

"Is that a baby carrier?" She laughs behind her coffee cup.

"It is the twenty-first century, D, men take care of their babies." My sarcasm is playful.

"Oh I know. But…" Her laugh is full and her smile reaches her eyes, "I just never thought I'd see you, rough and tough, wearing a sling with a baby in it."

I scoff at her, playing offended, placing my hand over my son's head. "This little guy makes me do crazy things." I wink at her which causes her demeanor to change.

Back in serious mode, "When will you be back? I have missed time to make up for."

"With me or Carter?" I can't help but take the opportunity to see if she still wants to stop our arrangement.

"Zach.." Her voice is low, full of sorrow and I know her answer without her saying it.

It is over.

"I'm just teasing D, I will have him back to you in about 45 minutes. Just finishing up the grocery shopping and we will be home. I have a meeting at one anyways." My tone starts out playful but is full of disappointment by the time I stop talking.

"See you soon."

An hour later I pull up to our cabin, my heart drops as a reminder that this isn't the family I envisioned passes through me. Danni opens the door and stands there with her hands on her hips. I know that she is joking, but any inclination that I have let her down leaves a sour taste in my mouth.

I hand her our son and head back to the car for the groceries. When I return she is sitting on the floor with her back against the couch, knees raised and singing to our son. It doesn't go unnoticed that the song she is singing is the same one Aunt Celia sang to us as kids.

At some point Carter falls asleep and she sits at the island with a baby monitor. I know she wants to ask about Brock, but is afraid of the answer. Erasing all the bad in her life isn't something I am capable of, but proving to her that I won't be one of those things is.

"Judge Masters will take care of it." I continue to place food in the pantry, while she sits behind me. "He put a rush on it, with all the medical records, photographs, and video recordings he will go away for a while. Each charge will be separate and non-concurrent." I finally turn to look at her, tears are streaming down her face. "You are safe D. He won't hurt you again."

She quickly wipes her face when she sees me looking, but doesn't break eye contact. "I didn't want anyone to know. I didn't want to be seen as weak."

"This isn't your fault. Fuck, if anything it is mine. I shouldn't have…" I stop talking, I am willing to accept the blame, but I don't want to give her the idea. Another reason to hate me, another wall I have to break down. "All that matters is he won't do it again. You won't ever have to worry about another man touching you again. Do you hear me? I won't let it happen?" I kiss her forehead as I walk out of the kitchen. She is going to need space to process and I have a meeting with a car.

I HAD HOPED to get quite a bit of work done on the car while Danni was away, but with the amount of thoughts that ran through my head, my hands were busy doing something else. Instead I use the excuse that she wants alone time to get out of the house without questioning.

"Took you long enough. Shit I figured you'd been out here all night." Garret has clearly been her a while, and by the way he is zooming around the garage I would guess he has drank at least four pots of coffee.

"Did you save any caffeine for the rest of the town?"

"Couldn't sleep. I had to talk myself out of going down to the jail at lease six times throughout the night." He cracks his knuckles, the anger still radiates off of him.

"We did what she wanted. She doesn't have the heart to take someone's life, even indirectly. She would have hated herself and us. It was the best way." I pat him on the shoulder and hand him the sand paper, "Put that energy to good use."

"Do you think we can finish this by Christmas? It would make one hell of a gift."

"That is the plan, it should help when your mom and dad get moved back. They will be able to distract her, then I can use all your time and free labor."

"Do you think it will work?"

"I don't know man. I fucked up. Fucked up bad. If it wasn't for me she would have never dated that prick."

"There is no way that you can blame yourself for his shitty actions. You did what you thought was best for her, and let's be honest, she has done some really great things. So have you by the way. Not that I am happy you were married to someone other than my sister, but you saved Liz. You have also changed the practices of your farm, anonymous or not, we know where the extra funding for the school comes from each year."

Garret is a great friend, the best, but it doesn't matter what he says or how many good deeds I do, it will never replace the bad that I have done to Danni.

Twenty-Eight

DANNI

Carter's first Thanksgiving went as expected, everyone fought for his attention in between naps, football played in the background, and love completely filled the home. I know he won't remember the gathering, but I will. It was a great way to see that Zach and I love our son enough that co parenting and being a family together is something we can do. It was a great day, but I know it won't always be that easy.

In the two weeks since the dinner life has been a bit awkward. Zach hasn't come on to me once, and truth be told I kind of miss it. The entire drive to Missouri I was rehearsing how I would tell him that what we were doing had to stop, but I didn't anticipate snapping at him and telling him to fuck off. I clearly jumped the gun and assumed that he was taking it upon himself to progress our relationship further than just sex and I lost it. I was just tired of him making decisions for me without a conversation, and I assumed it was the same actions and he learned nothing. I hate that I was wrong, I love that I was wrong.

I HAVE BEEN PACING the porch for thirty minutes arguing with a supply company that was supposed to have items for the study delivered last week. Being on maternity leave has left tasks to others, and I just can't rely on them. There have been way to many mistakes than I am comfortable with and I refuse to let my study fail because of someone else's error. I felt my blood pressure rising and my eye began to twitch, my sign that I needed to be outside so I didn't wake Carter.

"My study starts January first. How can I make that timeline if I don't have the damn supplies?"

"I am sorry ma'am. It looks like the boxes are stuck in a facility in San Antonio. Policy states if they are there for 14 days we can reship."

"I get your policy, but I have contacted the carrier and they can't find them. I filed a claim with them to expedite the process, but I can't wait another three days before you ship again. It is already the second week of December and the holidays are sure to add time. You do realize this is a United States Government funded program. You are hindering the job of a government employee." The only mistake this lady made today was answering my phone call. It isn't her fault that the carrier lost the packages, and I am sure she doesn't write the policies either, but someone has to take my wrath or shit won't get done. I am pissed and freezing, which increases my anger.

I didn't even hear the door shut or his boots cross the wooden planks of the porch, but the blanket being wrapped around my shoulders tips me off that he is here. He grabs the baby monitor out of my hand and replaces it with a cup of hot tea. Each action melts my heart, a heart that pushed his away and I don't know how to get it back.

"Why don't you let me talk to them? You go inside and warm up, I just started a fire." He is trying to calm the anger that is simmering inside me before I explode on an innocent bystander and I can't even act like I am fine. He knows all my tells.

"I can't. You don't have the pull I do with this kind of thing. I need the tubing and soil sample kits or I won't be able to work on the irrigation part of the study. If this study flops I won't be able to..." I haven't told him my plan, so I stop talking before I say too much.

"You won't be able to what Danni?" He is genuinely curious, but there is also a bit of his usual smolder and I love it, "You won't be able to stay her on the farm and see me every day?" His sarcasm and joking is a body armor, one that he thinks makes me believe he is okay with all of this, but I am no fool. Well I am, but it is because I pushed him away again instead of doing what my heart really wanted. He grabs the phone and pushes me inside, there is no use in me trying to fight it, I know I won't win.

Once inside I head straight to my room. The fire Zach started is nice, but when I am cold to my bones only a hot shower will truly warm me up. As I grab my towel from the linen closet a brown box falls. The brown box I hid after the festival, inside is a book with pages folded to reveal a beautiful hummingbird. A gift. A gift I don't know how to give without it being more than that, just a gift. Then it hits me, Mrs. Turner is my son's grandmother and he deserves to know about her and what she loved. I take the book out and carry it to the nursery. Carter is still asleep so I place the book on the shelf, and tell him a little story.

"My dearest son." My voice is quiet, and I check that he doesn't stir before I continue. "You my love have changed the world and you are just a baby. You entrance was a bit unconventional, but you my dear were made from love. I bought that book for your daddy, a reminder of a token from our past, but a way to honor your grandma as well. I don't think I am ready to admit it yet, at least not to anyone who can spill my secret, but I never stopped loving your daddy. I am just too stubborn to let him win this fight, at least right now. I do have a plan though. If this study does what I think it will, I plan to step back from research. Maybe do some work from home coding, maybe just farm, one thing is for sure I will always be your mommy. I will always love you, I just hope I get to do it with your daddy." I pat the side of his crib and leave the room.

The hot shower was just what I needed to warm up. I don't know how long I have been standing here, but I can't bring myself to move. The hot water doesn't just remove the cold from my bones, but the stress from my body as well. The knock on the door brings me back to reality and I see it opening before I answer.

"Hey, I just wanted to let you know that the supplies will be here tomorrow. They are going to overnight a shipment, no need to worry about the missing one. I am going to head out and check on some things in the barn, I put the baby monitor on the sink. Let me know if you need anything from town and I'll go get it."

The baby monitor, fuck! Did he hear what I told Carter? He couldn't have, he would have said something. There is no way that he would hear me confess my love for him and my plan to stay and not instantly want to talk about it. I clear my head enough to respond, "Thanks. I was thinking of making potato soup and grilled cheese. Can you check that we have all the ingredients before you go?"

"Sure, I'll text you when I am headed back." He turns to leave but pauses, "Hey Danni,"

"Yeah," fuck he knows and he is about to ruin everything. Or did I ruin everything?

"Nice ass!" The door shuts and I wish I could throw something at him.

Twenty-Nine

ZACH

I don't really have anything that I need to do in the barn, I just need to get the hell out of the house before I do something stupid. It took everything I have not to get the ring out of the safe and convince Danni to elope before she could change her mind. I can't do the one thing that she hated me for, make decisions for her instead of with her.

Now I am driving to town to grab a bag of potatoes and milk because I threw away the ones from the pantry. I didn't need to, I already told her I was leaving, but I panicked. I thought that I could get a bit of extra time away, but also still get to be there with her while she cooks. I know it is silly and most men wouldn't admit it, but there is nothing like cooking a meal with the person you love. Lately my experience has been different, I pretend to read or work at the island while she cooks, just to be near her. If I am cooking I act like a fool who overwhelmed himself and needs a bit of help. For someone as detail oriented as I am, I am surprised it is working.

As I drive I replay what I heard over the monitor in my head over and over again.

I never stopped loving your daddy.

... I just hope I get to do it with your daddy.

The thought of being a real family with Danni and Carter brings tears to my eyes. There isn't anything I wouldn't give to make it happen if it truly is what she wants. The chance at forgiveness, a second chance at being her husband, it is worth everything I have.

In my original plan to win Danni back I bought and rebuilt the Mustang, but now I feel like I may need a little less of a grand gesture and more of a slow burn. Christmas is just around the corner and it is the perfect excuse to get something without letting her know I know her secret. I stop in at the jewelers before I go to the market, I am thinking a sentimental gift that shows she is Carter's mom is the perfect first step. I will say it is a gift from Carter, but the thought and heart I put into it is from me and she will know it.

The cases are filled with beautiful one of a kind pieces, earrings, bracelets, necklace, and the engagement rings. That is one area I will never have to go, my grandmother's ring will always belong to Danni, even if she doesn't accept it from me. I find the area with birthstone pieces to begin my search, why are there so many different stones? There are only twelve months in the year, yet there are more than twelve stones. I have never been the type of guy to understand the hoopla of jewelry, I bought her the best diamonds and whatever caught her attention. Now there are birthstones and birth flowers, initials, and even horoscope items. There is nothing here that speaks to me, feeling defeated I turn towards the door. As I am about to leave something catches my eye, a case full of bracelets and charms. This is it. This is my way in.

I buy the gold bracelet and a few charms. A "C" for Carter, a horseshoe for Kash, but also selfishly hoping that it brings me good luck, and a hot air balloon to reminder her of our trip in New Mexico. It covers our son, a sentimental memory, and a fucking hot one as well. All the things I need her to remember.I also place an order for a few charms that they don't have in stock, but will be great to give to her as we build our story. I may be getting ahead of myself here, but this is keeping me from getting on one knee and getting shut down.

I am running my card when a notification on my phone tells me I have an email. It is shipping confirmation for the order that I placed for Danni's supplies. I don't have to pay for anything that has to do with the grant, but I wasn't about to let this continue to stress her out. I apologized to the person on the phone and asked them to create a new order with the same supplies and add overnight shipping.

I didn't apply for the grant for the same reason that most people did. They either wanted the fame that came with the study connected to Dannielle Graham, "Farm Tech Guru," or they have a struggling farm and want the opportunity for her skills to help save it. The free supplies, technology, and additional farm hands are a huge benefit as well. I however needed Danni, "Soul mate and mother of my child," to save me.

Danni has always been my safe spot. The year that Danni and I got close was the same year I tore my labrum and dislocated my shoulder at a rodeo in Texas. My arm was never the same and I knew I lost all chance of playing baseball in college, let alone the MLB. I was kicking straw mixed with horse shit, pissed that my arm had ruined my future and making me take longer on chores when I heard her giggle. Typically someone laughing at you failing and throwing a fit would piss you off, but it was the first time I relaxed in a week. It was also the first time I had looked at her as more than Garret's twin sister, a nerd with her nose always in a book.

She started helping me with my chores every day, and every day my anger about not playing baseball dissipated. Instead our rivalry for our favorite teams became what I cared about most. Danni and I both grew up in Northwest Missouri, but she has been a Cardinals fan her entire life. Even better she is just a true fan of baseball, and would watch any game. We watched hundreds of games together when we could or listened to them on the radio while doing chores, and as much as I love the boys in blue, they just can't hang with the redbirds.

My love for Danni grew tremendously that summer, but my love for baseball never went away. A few years back the summer collegiate baseball league was going through a slump. Attendance was down and sponsors weren't investing in the team any longer. When the owner came to me about the lack of funds and how he was going to have to leave the league I took the opportunity to purchase the team. The Briarville Broncos are an investment that I have been mostly a silent owner in and pay for someone else to be the face of the team.

I use the team as an opportunity to give back to the community. We provide internships for students interested in many careers in sports. We partner with the local hospital to include therapists and trainer programs as well. The young men we bring in to play for the team are recruited throughout the college season and may be local or travel from other areas of the country. For most it's the last time they will ever grace the diamond, but a few lucky ones make it into a MLB system. It is a great way to showcase our town and increase community involvement when they volunteer to house a player. It has been a tough climb, but the games sell out every year and we are raising another generation to love baseball.

CARTER IS LAYING in the playpen when I enter the house. It is set up in the living room, a perfect view from the kitchen where Danni stands chopping onions to soak for her soup. One thing I love about her is the way she attacks everything with a plan, even cooking dinner. Sitting on the butcher block counter is single dish for every ingredient she plans to use tonight. She already has the cheese unwrapped and stacked with each piece rotated just enough to keep it from sticking to the one underneath it. Opposite her and across the cutting board sits her trash bowl, one thing that isn't ever in the kitchen when I cook. Her clean as you go style is a world of difference from my "place it where there is open space and clean at the end" way of cooking.

I know I should keep things as they have been this last few weeks, but her words replay in my head and my heart tells me to jump. I know that she is definitely not ready to take that leap, so instead I try to initiate the just sex pact again. The only difference is I am not going to ask using my words, I know what she likes and I am goin to make her want me with more than just her heart.

I could easily set the groceries on the counter and walk away, but what fun would that be. I stand directly behind her, close enough to brush my body to hers as I reach around and place the bags on the counter. I lean in close and whisper into her ear, "You look fucking delicious. Her body tenses and she stops chopping the onions. I back away quickly and act like everything is normal and I didn't just cross a line. I can tell I've got her, she takes a second too long to respond.

"Excuse me?" She turns, her tone isn't accusatory, more curious as if she is trying to play off that she didn't understand me. I'll play.

"I said, this looks delicious." I smirk and wink.

"Oh," she almost sounds disappointed, "Thanks. It will be ready in about an hour. I still have to prepare the potatoes."

"I can peel them if you'd like."

"Not a chance," she points to the other side of the island, "when I cook you don't cross that line. I don't need the kitchen looking like the Tasmanian devil stopped by."

"That's fine, I got some work to do." I walk towards my office to get my computer and mumble, "the view is better from here anyway."

"What was that?"

"I said, I'll get my computer, right away."

When I return there is a raw potato sitting on a paper towel, the salt shaker, and a beer sitting on the island. Even after everything I have put her through, she still remembers the stupid small shit. I do wonder if she put it there because she cared or because she can't wait to make fun of me for eating a raw potato, the same way she laughed about it in the past.

The potatoes are boiling and Danni has cleaned everything except the pans she is currently cooking in when *At Last* by Etta James comes on the radio. For a moment she freezes, unsure how to react to the song that we planned on dancing to at our wedding. She doesn't look at me while she fumbles with the dish towel in her hand. It takes me three steps to get to her, but it feels like a mile. Slowly I grab the towel out of her hand and place it on the counter. I tip her chin so she has to look me in the eye, after a few seconds I extend my hand as an invitation to dance. My heart stops, fuck I hope she accepts.

After what feels like hours of agony she places her hand in mine. Taking advantage, I pull her close and wrap my arms around her. For the first time since she has been back we are interacting with our hearts and not just chasing an orgasm. I don't know when the song ended, it is the cries from the baby monitor that pulls us back to reality as. We stop dancing, but neither of us want to let go as *Yours* by Russel Dickerson tells the story of my life in the background.

"I.. uh.." I clear my throat and take a step back. "I'll take two sandwiches." She jabs at my shoulder and smiles. Thankful I didn't press the issue making it any more awkward than it already is. What she doesn't know, is that it isn't awkward for me. I leave the kitchen to take care of my son.

Thirty

DANNI

"I just don't know where we stand." I take a drink of my strawberry wine and point my toes to stretch my legs. Angela and I have been sitting here for hours, wrapping an excessive amount of presents for my four month old son. No one prepares you for the lack of self-control when it comes to buying for you kids. To be honest, I have no self-control no matter who I am buying for. Giving gifts provides me with so much more joy than receiving them.

"I told you this would happen." Her eyes never leave the wrapping paper as she talks. Wrapping is just another form of decorating for her, and it has to be perfect. She struggles to get the picture to line up and I see her focus in the way she scrunches her nose.

"Remind me to buy plain paper next year. That way you can focus on my problems instead of my presents."

"That would just be boring! Why be boring? We are not boring!" She is annoyed at just the thought, but laughs at they way I poke fun at her.

"We are two grown women sitting on a floor wrapping presents on a Saturday night. Sounds boring to me."

"Pshh! We've got wine, popcorn, and drama." Her eyebrows waggle as she draws out the last syllable of drama. A piece of popcorn leaves my hand and hits her on the forehead.

"But really, you're a mom. It is five days until your baby's first Christmas. You are living with the father of your child, who you are afraid to admit you still love. Even to me, which hurts a little if I am being honest. And now you are trying to decipher what kind of present to get him that says *thanks for being my kids dad and coparenting with me. I love you but I don't want anyone to know, but I do want you to know I don't hate you anymore."*

"I wouldn't say it needs to say all that. I just don't know what to get him. We have so much history that if I get him something he likes he will read into it, there will be some way to connect it to feelings. The only way to avoid that is to intentionally get him something he won't want, which he will read into it and think I still hate him."

"I know," she stands and heads towards the kitchen, I follow, "how about you give him courtesy."

"What?"

"Give him the truth Danni. You have been living under the same roof for weeks. Hell, you've even slept together since then. He has given you space, honesty, and most of all his love. Quit lying to yourself and everyone else, tell him the truth. You have a minimum of two years working together on this damn farm. You aren't leaving again, you wouldn't leave Carter, so you're back. We all know you're back even if you don't. Let him know he has you back, Danni. Admit you love him, and then tell him."

I am speechless, she is right, but I know my heart can't

take another breaking and it will shatter like glass if I try and fail at this. Plus the small flirtations for the last few weeks have reminded me of the way we used to be, the good times we spent together. Although the bad was a minute part of our relationship, it was the end of it and I can't take that again.

"All the presents are wrapped, at least the ones you have bought. I'm going to head home. Think about what I said. I'll see you at the B&B for the Christmas Eve Party. Don't fuck it up D."

FOR THE LAST forty-eight hours I tried to determine what to do with the conversation Angela and I had while wrapping presents. She is the only person I have spoke to about my gifting problem, but have been avoiding her since our conversation. I hate to admit she is right, and if I am around her it is exactly what I will do. Instead I have spent every moment I could with my mom. I forgot how great it felt having her so close and not having to spend quality time on FaceTime.

Yesterday we did some last minute Christmas shopping. Today we spent our morning baking our favorite treats and the afternoon delivering them to our friends around town. It was a great way to keep my mind busy and from overthinking about what my next step should be. Yet here I sit in the bathtub, soaking in hot water and my mind roaming to the man who causes sparks in my body.

It is Christmas Eve and I don't have a gift for him. There is absolutely nothing I could give the man that wouldn't cause him to overthink the meaning. He knows that I am purposeful with my gifts, and there is always a message. Right now my body is begging for pleasure, a message I am not sure my heart is willing to send.

There is only one way to ensure I don't act on my desires, self pleasure. The moment my eyes close I imagine his hands on my body and my center heats. I grab my waterproof bullet from the edge of the tub and rub it across my breast. Nothing is as good as him, no one ever has been. He knows how far he can push, how much I can take and the best way to make me come.

My left hand massages my breast, pinching my nipples while the toy in my right hand sends vibrations through my core. Pressure builds inside me, but I am still disappointed, this isn't how I want to spend the rest of my life. An orgasm is meant to be shared, something created from passion between two people. Fuck it, I turn off the toy and step out of the bath. I will never be truly happy living with the man I am in love with, especially if he doesn't love me back. It is time to stop being a coward and take a chance. Tonight I will give him courtesy.

The long sleeve red dress clings to my body in all the right places. A deep "v" neckline accentuates my breast while the full length slit exposes part of the willow tree tattoo that graces my thigh. Silver sparkles match the glint in my eyeshadow. It isn't the dress I initially picked for the Christmas Eve dinner at the B&B, but it is more likely to get the job done than the blue cocktail dress that still hangs on my bathroom door. My dark hair is pinned to one side, curls flowing on the opposite side of my slit. The dress, makeup, and hair were all planned to draw his eyes exactly where I want them. I finish the outfit with a pair of black heals and my diamond earrings that Zach gave me for graduation.

After checking myself in the mirror one more time I leave my room and head to the stairs. I don't know if Zach is ready for the party or already gone. We didn't talk about riding together, but it would make sense. There is no point in driving two cars to the same place and back. I don't see him in the living room, and I already took Carter to my parents at the main house, so I assume he is gone. My phone pings with a text.

Zach: Wanted to check on Carter before I left. Be there in just a few.

Me: Give him a kiss for me.

Me: Tell my mom and dad thanks again.

A white Christmas is random in this part of the state. Sometimes it will snow on Halloween and be sixty degrees on Christmas. This is one of those years. I am a bit thankful for the unusually warm December weather though, it allows me to prance around in this dress without a parka ruining my plan. A plan I keep running through my mind, wondering if it is the right thing to do. The longer I wait here in silence the more panic sets in. What if he likes what we have created with our coparenting? What he really just wanted the sex? What if he wanted more, but I ruined it by cutting him off during the fiasco with Brock? What if he doesn't want someone who is pathetic enough to get the shit beat out of her? My intrusive thoughts have my mind racing and telling me this is a mistake. I listen and head upstairs to change into the less revealing but still formal cocktail dress I bought with my mom the other day.

"My God, Danni…" His words stop me as I hit the half way point of the stairs. I turn around as his hand pulls across his mouth and moves to the back of his neck where he grips and tries to gather his thoughts. His lips are slightly parted and his tongue lightly brushes the bottom one before he pulls it into his mouth with his teeth. I feel the blush creeping up my neck and to my cheeks, it is working, and I'll be damned if I am changing now. A deep breath settles me, my inner voice tells me 'confidence is key, you're a queen, his queen.'

"Hello handsome. Would you mind grabbing my coat?" I do my best to keep the seduction in my voice and the nerves out.

"I'd rather take you out of that dress." His voice is deep and full of lust. He takes a step closer to me, reaches for my hand which I give him, and spins me around. "You look absolutely stunning D."

"Thank you, are you sure it isn't too much?" I fane shyness.

"You know what, it might be. Why don't we go upstairs and I will help you out of it." He laughs, but I can see the desire building in his pants.

"This is the first time I have been to Avery's for Christmas Eve in three years. You will not be the reason I miss it." I walk towards the door to grab my coat, but stop and look over my shoulder. "But who knows a few cocktails and I may be ready to come home early."

Zach is on my heels helping with my coat. "Well, let's get those drinks then."

Thirty-One

ZACH

I am not sure what is happening right now, but I know I don't want it to stop. Danni sits in the passenger seat of my truck talking about the gifts she bought Carter and how excited she his to celebrate Christmas the way she did growing up. However, that is all I can tell you. I can't focus on the details because all I can think about is the way she looks in that dress and how she acted like she wanted me. It didn't go unnoticed that she is wearing something completely different than what has been hanging on the closet door since her shopping trip with her mom or the fact that she is showing of her tattoo and breast. She wouldn't bring attention to that if she didn't want it.

I take her coat as we enter the foyer at Dogwood, any chance to get close to her, to touch her. She immediately begins to make her way to Angela and Avery who stand near the fireplace. I however make my way to the bar to get her started on the cocktails, my apparent countdown to getting her out of that dress and into my bed.

"Whiskey and a Chocolate Paradise please."

"This is not how I expected to find you tonight." Garret moves into the spot beside me.

"And how was that?" I am curious to know if there is a plan I am not a part of or if I am just that pathetic.

"Well not ordering my sister's drink. Aren't you on some weird coparenting kick where neither of you do anything that might expose your feelings for the other?" He smirks, then takes a swig of his drink, which I assume is bourbon based on the smell.

"Yeah, I thought so. Then she comes out looking like a grown man's dream and saying shit that I can't decipher." I release a sigh and down my whiskey. "I'm going to need another one of these please."

"Slow down cowboy. And don't talk about your sex dreams that involve my sister anymore okay."

"Fuck off dude!" We laugh and make our way towards the girls.

I wait until Danni is done hugging her brother before I hand her the martini glass. As much as I'd love to see the drink spilled down his back has he spins her it just means I'd have to wait longer to get her to leave. Danni mingles and drinks a few more cocktails before she gets the honor of placing the star on the top of the tree. Avery picks someone new every year, and I am not surprised that after years of not making it home, Danni is picked tonight. Her movement is limited by her dress and her ability to climb the step stool is hindered, as is my ability to breath. The old stool wobbles a bit and she pauses to steady it, but my hands go straight to her hips. There isn't a chance in hell that I would let her fall. When she feels my hands on her hips she turns and looks down at me with a smile that reaches her eyes and winks. She places the star and purposely falls back into my arms, demanding I catch her. I don't know what is more affected, my heart or my dick. I place her on the ground and she leans in close enough I can feel her breath as she whispers, "take me home." I can't help but feel that the meaning of that one word, home, is the same as it was six years ago.

The drive home is nothing like the drive there. Danni doesn't speak, she leans into the center console instead of the door. She connects her phone to the bluetooth and begins playing her favorite Christmas songs. She is at home, and she is letting me know it. Each action is a secret spilled, a promise, an olive branch, and I want the whole damn tree. When I pass the house but don't stop she looks at me with confusion plastered on her face. I give her a crooked smile and head straight to the old barn where a jet black 1967 Fastback sits, ready to be gifted. I park the truck and remove my tie to use as a blindfold, then make my way to her side of the truck.

"Zach, what is going on? Why are we at the barn in the middle of the night, and why the hell am I blindfolded."

"You aren't the only one with surprises tonight." I lace our fingers together and walk backwards to lead her inside. "I am sorry I lied to you."

"I don't know what is going on, but I don't like the way this is starting."

"It isn't what you think. I promise. Now stand here and don't remove the blindfold until I say." I grip the tarp in my hands to reveal the car once she can see. "Okay, ready?"

"Zach, you better not be fucking with me."

"Oh I'm going to fuck you honey, just not yet. One.... Two.... Three!" My tie is in her hand and I whip the tarp off, revealing my dream girl's dream car. Her hands immediately cover her mouth and a tear rolls down her face.

"Is this..."

"You bet your ass it is! Your brother and I rebuilt it. I

wasn't sure you'd be ready to accept something from me, so I made sure it was never in my name. I put it in Carter's name so I could keep it a surprise and still get it road ready for you. Wanna take it for a spin?"

"Fuck yes, but I have had too much schnapps to get behind the wheel." Before I know it her lips are on mine. She pulls away to thank me and walks towards the hood of the car. She leans over the hood and splays her arms out as if giving the car a hug. "It isn't a mom car, but I'd be lying if I said I didn't want it."

The moment she turns my lips crash into her, my hands grip her ass and sit her on the hood. My cock throbs with every touch, her hands grip the hair at the base of my neck, and the sexiest moan I have ever heard breaks free from her lips. Merry Fucking Christmas to me.

My knees hit the ground as I place her legs on my shoulders to kiss and nip at her thighs. The slit of her dress provides for some flexibility, but not enough. I pull her hips down towards my face and push her dress higher revealing her black lacy thong. This is the moment I decide how the rest of this is going to play out. I want to show her my feelings, that I love her, that I need her, remind her that this is what life is supposed to be. I just don't know that on the hood of the car is the best way to do that. I ache for her, for her release, for her sounds and that I know I can make happen here.

I rip the thin fabric that covers her core and shove it up with the dress. My fingertips tease with soft touches everywhere but where she wants them and her hips squirm beneath me.

"Please, Zach I am begging you." Her breath is raspy and causes a growl to escape from me.

"What is it that you want Sweetheart?" I won't just give

in, we have too much history and competing to control the bedroom is a fun game we like to play.

"More."

"Say it. Tell me what you want. You have to tell me sweetheart." I use my beard to scratch her inner thigh, goosebumps spread across her skin.

"Fuck me."

"How, baby?'

"Damnit Zach, I don't care how you fuck me, I just need you to do it."

"Already conceding Darlin? That was a quick round." I chuckle then swipe my tongue over her folds. Her hips push into my face, her body needing more.

"I have lifetime to enact my revenge. Now use your tongue for better purposes." Her hand grips my hair, pulling it towards her and I give in. I grip her ass and hold her to my mouth, devouring every juice that drips from her. My fingers slide inside her, pumping hard while my tongue massages her clit. Her body starts to shake and I work her through the first of many orgasms I plan to give her tonight.

Once her body relaxes on to the hood of the car I stop lapping her with my tongue. I stand with remnants of my prize still glistening in my beard. "I was right, you are delicious." A smirk crosses my face as she realizes my comment from the other night. I reach out my hand to pull her to her feet. She stumbles into my arms and smashes her lips to mine. The kiss feels like heaven and I don't ever want to stop. When she pulls away to catch her breath I spin her around and remove her dress, with one hand around her waist I pull her ass to me while my other hand pushes her chest to the hood. "Don't move.

"I lied too, you know." Her words are baiting me. " I don't deserve the car." I don't gift her with a verbal response, instead I drop my slacks and boxer briefs to my ankles and thrust into her from behind.

"You deserve everything you get Sweetheart." I growl and my hand lands a firm smack on her ass. Caught off guard, her body jumps, but then shoves back towards me, asking for more. I rub the red spot to sooth the area before I smack again. "Quiet isn't an option baby, stop holding back. Let the whole farm know you are mine." I smack again.

"Fuuuuuck! Is that all you got? I remembered it better." He words give me permission to keep going. I lean over her body and wrap my hands around her, one hand squeezes her breast, pinching and teasing, while the other wraps firmly around her throat.

"Don't ask for something you aren't ready for D!" My teeth dig into her shoulder and her moans have my balls aching for release. I stand up, positioning her for the ride she is about to get. Her long hair is now wrapped around my right hand as I pull her head back exposing her neck. I drag my tongue from her shoulder blade to her ear, where I bite before saying, "Don't come until I give you permission."

Her hands fight for a grip on the hood as her body responds to mine thrusting into her. I support her weight as her legs begin to weaken, but her screams get louder.

"That's it baby, come for me." She releases control and her body shakes as her pussy surrounds my cock like a vice. It is all it takes for me to reach my breaking point, with one last thrust I explode inside her. "As always, D. As, always."

Thirty-Two

MARCH

DANNI

My team surrounds the large table in the loft of the barn, the space we designated as our meeting space. It is early spring and one of the busiest times for the team. We are prepping the equipment for the irrigation, even though we are not studying the impact on different irrigation methods, our method is a constant variable that we need in place. I want to be sure everything is ready and working before Zach and his hands plant in May.

"Are you sure taking on so many different aspects isn't too much? This is the same as five studies in one, but we still only have one team." Greg is the one person who always questions my ability and I always prove him wrong. He feels that he got shafted in a few different areas 'because I am a woman' and instead of arguing with him, I let my talent and product speak for itself.

"If I didn't think it would work, I wouldn't do it." I don't look at him as I flip through pages in the file. "The point of the study is to test our program on as many aspects of farming as possible. Turner Farms gives us the opportunity to do so. After the study we will have a clear picture of what we can and can't do, we will be able to market it correctly." When I look up to accompany my words with an assertive look I catch a glimpse of Zach leaning against a post with a smirk on his face. He doesn't join the meetings often, he trust me and my team to do what is best, as a matter of fact I think the only reason he comes is to see me. We have kept our relationship secret since the Christmas Eve party. We don't want to give the board any reason to believe that I chose Turner Farms for the wrong reason. It has proven harder than expected, especially as he stands across the room with the same grin on his face he had this morning after he ate me for breakfast.

"But…" Greg starts to argue with me once again, but I don't allow it.

"Your assignments for the week are in your folder. I expect each of you to be thorough as Mr. Turner and I will both be checking in with each of you. This study is important to us, but this farm is his livelihood. Remember that my number isn't for emergencies only, I would rather you ask questions before making a decision you are unsure of."

My team files out of the loft with goodbyes, but Zach stands still waiting until the last person leaves the barn. He swiftly moves towards me, a hunger in his eyes. "You are real fucking sexy when you take charge." His voice is low and I don't know if it is because he doesn't want to be heard or if he is trying to hide his desires.

"You already knew that, I have controlled you for ages." I laugh as I begin to organize the papers that still sit in front of me.

"I'm not the only one that feels that way. Greg looks at you like you are the reason for his wet dreams."

"I'm sorry, do I hear a hint of jealousy in your voice Mr. Turner?" I poke fun, but there is absolutely no reason for him to be jealous Greg, the man who hates that he is assigned to my team and that I am in control. "I can assure you that the only dream that Greg has of me is him pushing me off a roof and him running away with my accolades."

"Maybe I am wrong, I don't really care either way. He can dream of you all he wishes, I am the one making you come nightly. More than once." He shrugs his shoulders like he is proud of himself. "Speaking of, what time will you be done today. Your mom wants us to come to the main house for dinner, but I'd like to start with appetizers in the cabin."

"Zachary Ryan, is that all you think about?"

"Mostly, sometimes I think about the farm. The rest of my day my mind is focused on you and Carter. For very different reasons."

"Today is going to be a late night. Tell my mom we can be there for dinner at seven, but you will have to settle for dessert."

"I can handle that." He kisses my forehead and walks away.

THERE IS a miscommunication between the sensors on the time domain reflectometry and the irrigation system in the test area. The irrigation is turning on when the soil moisture levels are too high and not turning on when they are low. I am supposed to be finding the error in Molly's coding that is causing my program on the irrigation system to not work. I have been staring at the computer screen for two hours, but my mind is preoccupied and I can't focus. I am worried about the board finding out about Zach and I. It has only been three months and I have a long time left to hide. I don't want to hide anymore though, Zach doesn't deserve to be a secret I have to keep. People are also starting to ask about Carter and his father, that is one thing about Zach I will never hide. I know what I have to do, and if it cost me the study I am okay with it. My family has to be my priority.

"Hey Jane, thanks for picking up after hours."

"I'm an attorney, I don't have after hours." Jane is very matter of fact, knows her shit, and is worth every dime I have ever paid her.

"I have a bit of a situation and I am wondering how it will impact my company, my study, and my business partnership with the USDA."

"I'm all ears."

"The farm I picked for the study was the best option. The board vetted all the applications prior to sending them to me, and then I picked the finalist. However, when I did I failed to mention that the owner, well soon to be owner, is the father of my child."

"I didn't know you had a child."

"Well, funny story, neither did I. My ex and his widow did IVF. There was this huge mix up and they used my eggs instead of hers, small towns right. Anyways, Carter, my son, is nine months old. And though I picked the farm based on the best application, it may not look like that to outsiders."

"I can work with this, should be no problem. I can put a call in tonight." Her confidence is reassuring, but she doesn't have all the facts.

"You should also know that after finding out about my son, I worked through some shit with people here at home. His father and I have been coparenting for the last five months, and all those feelings are coming back." I pause for a moment to breath and decide how I am going to play this. "I can't lie to you Jane…"

"Maybe you should lie to me Dannielle. I am your attorney." She interrupts.

"That isn't who I am, my integrity is important to me, but so is my family and that is why I am calling you. I want this study to continue and I want to be a part of it, but if that means hiding my family, the people I love, I won't do it. I need to know if you can help me keep the study when I tell the board that Zachary Turner is the father of my child and I am in love with him."

"I'll do what I can. Let me make that call and I will get back to you."

"Understand this Jane. I will tell them. I won't hide my relationship with Zach any longer. We have been through too much shit and I'd rather have him than this study."

"Understood." She disconnects the call and I place my phone on the desk. My hands scrape down my face as I let out a deep breath. I know what I am doing is right. Zach sacrificed for me when he called off the wedding, and I will do that for him now, for us. As I look up I see the greatest image that I could ever be blessed with. Zach is standing in the door way with a bottle of wine and two prepackaged cupcakes. His smile reaches his eyes and he walks into the office.

"I didn't have enough time in the last three minutes for anything else." I give him a questioning look. "It has been almost seven years since I have heard you declare your love for me to anyone. I think that calls for a celebration."

"It's true. Zachary Ryan Turner, I am in love with you. I want the world to know it and if we can't do the study I will pass it on. You are what matters. You and Carter."

Thirty-Three

JULY

ZACH

One of the Briarville Bronco's interns just finished a beautiful rendition of the national anthem and my palms have started sweating. It is the home opener for the team, and Danni thinks we are just normal community members supporting the local team. She isn't ready for the amount of information that she is about to receive. Kacen, the woman I have hired as the face of the Bronco's walks to home plate to give a speech like she never has before.

"Good evening Briarville! Welcome to our season opener. I know you all are excited to meet the players this evening, but the Broncos have a little surprise for you. Over the last five years there have been many changes here at Thompson Stadium, one being ownership. Under this ownership our team as moved from nearly leaving the league to multiple championship rings. I know that many of you see me and think that I am responsible for these changes, but you couldn't be more wrong. I just get paid to look like it. So I would like to welcome our owners to the field at this time. Please give a huge welcome to Zach Turner and Danni Graham along with their son Carter."

Danni stares at me befuddled, unsure of what to do, I place my hand on her lower back and lead her out to the field. Kacen hands me the microphone and shakes my hand before she hugs Danni and walks off the field. I let the cheers quiet down before I speak.

"Thank you, thank you very much. Baseball has always been a huge part of my life and part of the reason this woman is standing next to me. I even dreamed of playing for the Broncos before my injury. After my injury I was broken and angry. I didn't know how my life could be worth anything without baseball. Then one day my friend's sister showed me that there is so much more to baseball than playing, then so much more to life than baseball. She saved me. I have made many mistakes in the years that we spent together, the biggest one was letting you walk away." I turn to her and wipe the tear that is rolling down her cheek with the pad of my thumb. "I am not saying I won't make mistakes in the future, but I won't ever be the reason you walk away again. I thought I was broken at 15, but living without you was the most broken I have ever been." I drop to one knee as I pull my grandmother's ring, Danni's ring out of my pocket. "Dannielle Graham, you have been the love of my life, my savior, the mother to my child, please make me the luckiest SOB in the world and be my wife too."

DANNI

There are 5,000 people staring at me as I stand on the field holding my son and the only person I ever loved is on one knee asking me to marry him for the second time. Everything in me knows this is what life is supposed to be, our farm full of kids and animals, giving back to the community. When the hell did he buy a baseball team? Get it together Dannielle, put the man out of his misery. I can't speak, so I just nod. Before I realize it my mom is taking Carter from my arms, I don't even know where she came from. Zach is placing a ring on my finger, his grandmother's ring. A ring he never let anyone else wear despite me leaving. The crowd erupts into cheers and whistles and At Last blares throughout the stadiums PA system.

"I love you Zachary!" It is the only thing I manage to get out before his lips crash into mine. When we come up for breath he places his strong hands on each side of my face and touches his forehead to mine.

"As Always."

Epilogue

DANNI

I am sitting on the loveseat in our bedroom with my hair wrapped in a towel and another wrapped around my body. The baby monitor is sitting on end table beside my tea. I am reviewing the book I wrote on the study at Turner Farms. I knew a book would follow, and when Jane was able to help me keep the study despite being in love with the owner of the farm, I knew I wanted to complete it as soon as possible. I kept very detailed notes and wrote chapters as the data was provided. I was able to send the book to editing within four weeks of completing the study. This is my final review and with my approval we will send to publishing.

Sunday mornings are the best time for me to read and relax. My mom and dad take their grandkids to breakfast and spend the day with them every week. Mylah is only two months old so I keep her home with me, but she is a great sleeper. Zach is taking flying lessons from Garret every Sunday, and I am pretty sure he is going to try and convince me to buy a plane. My life after the study is different than it had been for the three years prior, but it is what I always thought it would be. I have been writing a business plan for permanent STEAM camps in our county and those that surround it. I have also started a scholarship fund for girls who are pursuing technology careers. I had a dedication ceremony for Aunt Celia to honor all she had done for me, and it was one of very few times I saw the strongest woman I know cry.

A soft knock on the door breaks my attention from the book. “I just wanted to let you know I was heading out to the strip. Do you need anything before I go?” Zach is the doting father and husband that I knew he would be.

“I think I am good. Thanks though. Fly safe and come home to me.” It is the same sentence I say every Sunday. I love my brother and husband, but flying small engine planes terrifies me.

He kneels down in front of me and eases his hands up under my towel. “I will always come home to you. To Carter. To Mylah.” He hand moves to lift my ankle and his lips follow. His kisses progress up my leg to my inner thigh. The tickling from his beard causes me to giggle.

“Don’t you have lessons to go to?”

“Mmmhmm.” He pulls the towel, exposing my body to him. “Damn you’re sexy.”

“Then what are you doing?” I laugh knowing he has already lost control of his ability to walk away. He will be late to the strip today.

“Fucking my wife.”

Want More Briarville?

If you enjoyed reading Danni and Zach's story be on the look out for more love in Briarville. You can read the first chapter of Becoming Yours, the story of Angela and Oliver right here.

Keep up to date on all things Briarville and Emery Thompson by visiting my website at emerythompsonauthor.com and follow me on TikTok @ EmeryThompsonWrites.

Becoming Yours

PROLOGUE

Four Years Ago

ANGELA

I had the Uber drop me at the market instead of the apartment. I know that Tyler will be working late, but it is our anniversary and he deserves a home cooked meal to come home to. It won't be anything fancy, I am a country girl and I cook like it. We will probably be able to eat leftovers all weekend from the one casserole. Actually, that is my plan: make a hefty meal and snack on it in between all the orgasms, never having to leave the apartment.

"That will be $56.32." The cashiers voice brings me back from a the mental image of Tyler between my legs as I am spread on the kitchen counter. I swipe my card and thank her before I step out on to the busy sidewalk of New York. The apartment is six blocks away and the night is young, at least in New York. I should have plenty of time to get to the apartment and get dinner made before Tyler arrives.

"Good evening Mrs. Carpenter." The door man smiles as

he welcomes me into the building. Butterflies fill my stomach as I still am not used to being called Mrs. Carpenter. Finding Tyler in Tahiti was a dream come true and a whirlwind romance.

My best friend Danni and I were on one of our yearly girl trips when we were influenced by the rum to crash a wedding. We didn't know where to sit, but there were more empty seats on the grooms side so we jumped at the opportunity. Tyler was the best man, and I can't even tell you what the bride looked like due to my hyper focus on him. He was wearing the same cream colored tux as everyone else standing there, but the green from his tie and pocket square matched his eyes and his deep brown skin stood out among the others.

As the wedding party exited the area he met my eyes, a crooked smile told me everything I needed to know. I was going to the reception area even if I had to drag Danni there. Six months later we eloped, and now we are about to celebrate our first wedding anniversary.

"Hello, George." I reach in and give him a hug. It took me a few months to get him to hug back, but now it is like second nature. George has worked for the building since he was twenty-two providing his wife and three daughters with the income they need to survive. Now he brings his grandkids to visit this side of town each week to tell them the story of true love and the struggle to win the approval of the heiress's father. A story of love conquering all, even being cut off from all financial security. "I'll bring you down a plate of my famous chicken casserole later this evening." I kiss him on the cheek and head towards the elevator.

The elevator ride to the 32nd floor seems to take forever. I fidget with my keys as nervousness sinks in. I am want to make Tyler dinner for him to come home to, but I am also okay with jumping on him as soon as I walk in the door. I guess we will see what the plan is when I enter our part time getaway.

The bell rings letting me know I have reached my floor. With my groceries in one and and my keys in the other I nearly run to the door. I hear music playing through the door, either he is off work early or he forgot to turn off the radio, the latter being more likely. I insert the key to unlock the deadbolt and push open the door.

Emotions rage through me.

Anger.

Disgusts.

Sadness.

Her long brown hair is wrapped around his wrist and he yanks it back while his other hand grips hip. She braces herself on the arm of the couch, completely naked except for the thigh high black leather stilettos. Her dark brown skin matches his, and only separates when he slides out before thrusting back into her.

"More, Tyler I fucking want more." She begs through her moans. He pulls her hair back and leans forward, dragging his tongue from the base of her neck to her ear where he whispers something I can't hear. She nods her head and he releases her hair.

His hands slide down her body, until he reaches where her back meets her ass. He pulls out of her, this time he doesn't thrust back in. He kneels down and spreads her ass with his hands, then begins to lick her pussy. His moans are guttural.

"Do you like that baby? Is it better than hers?" This bitch knows he is married and is still fucking him. I should leave, I should just turn around and go, but I can't. This is like a train wreck and I need to know his answer.

He stands up and smacks her ass. "I told you not to talk about her. Or do you like being punished?'

Her ass pushes towards him, she's playing a game. She is fucking my husband and I am just a game to them. He smacks her again, then pushes her over the couch and thrusts into again. This time he also shoves his thumb inside her ass. She moans, thanking him, begging him to not stop.

He smacks her again, and my hand twitches because I want to do the same thing to his face. Her though, I'd like to break her jaw.

I sit the bags down by the door, they are too engrossed in their fucking to notice the sound. Or maybe they don't hear it over the music in the background. Either way, they are about to notice me.

"Hey there, baby. Is this my gift?" He freezes mid thrust. I have never been attracted to a woman, but if I can turn this on her… Make her feel like the belittled bitch that she is I will. "Thanks for getting her primed and ready for me. I'll go get the strap on and we can really start having fun."

I walk to the bedroom to keep up the act, "Happy first anniversary, Tyler." I don't give them time to react, maybe she will actually be into it and plan on staying. I don't give two fucks. She can think I am getting ready for her, but truth is I am in the safe, taking the cash, my jewelry, and packing a suitcase of what belongings I do have here.

When I open the door she is standing in the kitchen with a robe and he has pulled his briefs back on. He stands in the middle of the living space, between her and me, unsure of which way he is supposed to go. She was fine with fucking him, knowing he was married, so why is she so bent out of shape now that I am here.

"Don't worry sweetie, he's all yours." My confidence is for show, inside I am breaking and I have to get out of this apartment before I crumble in front of them. "I'll call the moving company tomorrow. Should have your stuff by the end of the week." I dial a number as I walk to the door, when I place it on speaker phone and Zach answers, Tyler's face is overcome with fear. "Hi Zach. I just wanted to let you know that the population of Briarville has decreased by one tonight. Can you please go to my house and change the locks. I'm going to catch the next flight home. Oh and Zach, if he ever comes within three counties I want him to experience the Turner Law." I close the door and walk to the elevator.

I am thankful George isn't there to see me exit the building. I make it to the cab before I let a tear fall. I don't want to unload in the backseat of a strangers car making them uncomfortable so I focus on getting a flight. Once I book the ticket I call Danni.

OLIVER

I sit in the corner of Matty's and take another swig of my beer. The lights are low and the crowd begins to thin as last call approaches. She sits at a table with Turner and the pilot, Garret I think his name is, and the friend that can't keep her eyes off of him. There is something different this time, this isn't their typical Friday night. Usually there is laughter, darts, pool, and shots. Usually her husband is here. She's giddy and in love, taken.

The first time I saw her she was trying to unlock her bakery door with her hands full. I was passing by in a rush to get to the hardware store. The papers fell out of her hands and began to fly away, she panicked, but I stopped them. When my eyes met hers, my heart stopped. She was beautiful. Her blonde hair was braided and swept over her right shoulder. He blue eyes matched my view of Lake Michigan, and the way she bit her bottom lip sent shockwaves through my body.

It wasn't until I placed her papers in her hand and the rock on her left hand sparkled in the sun as she covered them to avoid it all happening again, that I realized there was no chance.

She's changed. Her smile is forced. She only dances with her girl friends or the same two guys anytime I see her at the bar. She never kisses them, it's never sexual with them. They are her protectors, they keep the other guys from asking her to dance. They are her walls and I don't know if any man will ever be able to tear them down. The girls are different. Sometimes it's hot, but it is never because she makes it that way. They get drunk and the one girl is trying to get the attention of the pilot.

The ring is gone. I don't know how long it has been gone, but I have been here for work for two weeks of every month for the last two years and this is the first I have seen it off. You can still see the tan line on her finger.

What did he do to her? How did he break her? I haven't seen him around town either. She's the local, he was the outsider, but everyone still loved him. How do they feel about him now? How could he break a woman like that and still be alive. I bet Turner had him killed. He is very protective of his community, of his family.

She has never noticed me, even on the day I met her. She was clearly in love with her husband and her eyes didn't wander. But I notice her. I notice the way her hips move causing my cock to strain against my jeans. I notice the dullness in her eyes where there once was sparkle, and even though I don't have a reason to, it makes my heart ache. I notice her passion for her bakery every time I walk by, but don't have the balls to walk in. I'm not a home wrecker, I know what is like to be betrayed. I intentionally stayed away from her, something has always drawn me to her, but I fought it, only allowing myself in the same room when she was with her husband or Turner.

Now it's different. Now I can start tearing down walls.

Acknowledgments

Writing my first novel was a journey that I never thought that I would be able to experience. Now I know that I couldn't have done it without the amazing support of all those that believed in me. A huge thanks to my husband who supported me through every step without knowing a single detail of the story. My best friend, Angela, who read as I wrote and was my #1 fan the entire way. My niece, Joslin, who helped me put myself out there on TikTok despite my fears. I also want to thank those who followed my journey through TikTok or my website, trusting a stranger to deliver is hard to do. Writing Danni and Zach's story reminded me of the dreams I had and now because of you all I have accomplished them.

Much Love,

Emery

About the Author

Emery Thompson is an emerging author of romance. She lives in Missouri with her husband and three children. She enjoys spending time outdoors and watching baseball. The Briarville Series is her first published work.

You can follow her writing journey at www.emerythompsonauthor.com or follow her on TikTok at EmeryThompsonWrites

Printed in the USA
CPSIA information can be obtained
at www.ICGtesting.com
LVHW020706120923
757078LV00005B/24

9 798988 723806